FOCUS ON THE FAMILY®

SIERRA JENS W9-BML-407

# Don't You Wish

## ROBIN JONES GUNN

BETHANY HOUSE PUBLISHERS
MINNEAPOLIS, MINNESOTA 55438

A Focus on the Family book published by
Bethany House Publishers
A Ministry of Bethany Fellowship International
11400 Hampshire Avenue South, Minneapolis, Minnesota 55438
www.bethanyhouse.com

Printed in the United States of America by
Bethany Press International, Minneapolis, Minnesota 55438

**Library of Congress Cataloging-in-Publication Data**

Gunn, Robin Jones, 1955–
    Don't you wish / Robin Jones Gunn.
       p. cm. — (The Sierra Jensen series ; #3)
    Summary: When Sierra meets Christy Miller and the gang at the beach party of
the century, she realizes that it's important to be careful what you wish for.
    ISBN 1–56179–486–4
    [1. Wishes—Fiction. 2. Sisters—Fiction. 3. Christian life—Fiction.] I. Title.
II. Series: Gunn, Robin Jones, 1955–
PZ7.G972Do 1996
[Fic]—dc20                                    96–11667
                                             CIP
                                             AC

00  01  02  03  04  /  15  14  13  12  11  10  9

To Sandra Byrd and Christine Suguitan,
fellow writers and God lovers,
who join me in The Three-Fold Cord

# chapter one

"**C**OME ON, BRUTUS, HELP ME OUT HERE, buddy. I know you can't wait to get to the park, but you have to hold still." Sierra pushed away her St. Bernard's attempt to deliver a slobbery kiss and cinched the leash around his massive, furry neck. "Now remember what I said about being on your best behavior around Amy and her dog. She'll be here any minute, and I don't want you drooling all over her car's backseat."

Brutus returned Sierra's gaze with droopy, brown eyes as he panted expectantly.

"Don't give me that innocent look," Sierra said, as she sat down on the floor of the front hallway and tugged on her old cowboy boots. "I'm serious. The only way to make a friend is to be a friend, and that's your job today. Be nice, okay?"

*Am I talking to Brutus or to myself?* Sierra wondered. Ever since Amy had asked Sierra if she wanted to go to the waterfront park on Saturday morning, she had been a little nervous. Making new friends in Portland had not come easily to her. Amy Degrassi was the closest thing

*1*

Sierra had to a friend here, and she didn't want to blow it.

"There's the doorbell. Let's go, Brutus." That's all it took to persuade the big fur ball to take off.

Sierra grabbed his collar and opened the front door. Dark-eyed Amy met her with a laugh. "You weren't kidding! He is a monster."

"We don't have to take him if you don't want to," Sierra said, pulling hard on the leash to keep Brutus from knocking Amy over in his exuberance to get outside.

"I think he would be fiercely disappointed," Amy said.

Sierra followed Amy to her car, a 1986 Volvo with a badly peeling paint job. On the backseat, with twig-like paws pressed against the window, was Peanut, Amy's itty-bitty Chihuahua.

"He's no bigger than a rat!" Sierra said. "I don't think this is such a good idea, Amy. I'm afraid Brutus is going to squish him. Or eat him."

"They'll be fine. Look, Peanut, I brought you a new friend."

Sierra expected the miniature dog to turn tail and look for a place to hide. Instead, he yipped merrily, clawing at the closed window. Brutus pressed both his paws on the glass and studied his new companion. He turned to give Sierra a look, which she imagined meant, "Is this a joke? You expect me to hang out with this little leftover?" But Brutus barked without malice, and when Amy opened the door, he even waited for Peanut to hop off the seat before he bounded inside.

"See?" Amy said. "They're going to be great friends."

Sierra's amazement didn't cease as they drove off and headed for the Burnside Bridge. She peeked over her shoulder and saw the two unlikely companions sniffing each other and making all the right kinds of amiable dog motions.

"I never would have guessed," Sierra said, turning back around. As she did, a tangle of her long, curly blond hair caught in the headrest. "Ouch!"

"Ouch?"

"My hair got caught."

"I hate when that happens," Amy said, tossing her wavy, dark hair over her shoulder. "I'm ready to chop mine off. I wish I had Vicki's hair—straight and sleek."

Most of the girls at school wished they had hair like Vicki's. Not to mention a face, body, and personality like hers. She was the kind of person that made people, especially guys, stop to look twice.

"Don't you hate having naturally curly hair?" Amy asked.

"Yes," Sierra said, tugging the locks from the metal bar and leaving several strands behind. The truth was Sierra had given up wishing her hair was different. Cutting it only made it curlier. Living in the moist climate of Portland, Oregon, only made it curlier. Every kind of curl-taming spray she had ever used only made it curlier. She had decided long ago to let it just go wild.

"I think Vicki is interested in Randy," Amy said. "Did he say anything to you about her?"

"No, why would he? Randy has barely spoken to me this week."

"Why isn't he talking to you?" Amy asked as she eased into a parking place along a side street. She pulled out her ashtray and sorted through the coins. "I thought you guys were buddies."

"I don't know. I'd like to think so. Here, I have some money."

Sierra opened her backpack and pulled out three quarters for Amy.

In the backseat, both dogs were eagerly barking and yipping.

"Okay, okay," Sierra said. "You boys get out the side door. And mind your manners, Brutus." She opened the back door slowly, tangling with Brutus's leash until she had a firm grip. Amy put the coins into the meter as Peanut ran around her feet in circles.

"Are you excited about your trip next week?" Amy asked.

"Yes, I'm really looking forward to it." Sierra kept her answer nice and tame. Actually, she was so excited that the last two nights she had had a hard time falling asleep. She had been thinking about her friends Christy Miller, Katie, Tracy, Todd, and Doug. She hadn't seen them since they were together in England three months ago. With Easter vacation around the corner, Sierra had big plans to hop on a plane and fly to Southern California to spend the week with them. But she toned down her answer because she didn't want Amy to think she was so wrapped up in those friends that she wasn't in the market for a few new ones.

"I wish I were going somewhere fun," Amy said, dropping the last coin into the meter. "It's going to be pretty uneventful around here."

"Brutus!" Sierra cried. He had run out of patience during their small talk and taken off across the grass at a gallop, with Sierra sailing behind him at the end of his leash. Not to be outdone, Peanut yipped wildly, tippy-tap-toeing his way after them.

Brutus flew across the long stretch of grass and came to a screeching halt in front of the water fountain. This downtown Portland landmark was designed with several circles of holes bored into the concrete sidewalk. The holes shot arcs of water 10 or more feet into the air before they all convened in the center. It wasn't a particularly warm April morning, yet a few kids were dodging in and out of the watery spires, trying to weave their way through the open spaces before the water pattern changed and the kids got soaked.

"Don't even think of it, Brutus," Sierra said, pulling him back toward the walkway. They waited for Amy and Peanut to catch up, and then Sierra and Amy tried to walk along the waterfront like normal people out for a Saturday stroll on a fine spring morning. Such an activity proved impossible.

Brutus galloped ahead despite Sierra's trying to slow him down. Peanut, not willing to be outdone, sprinted. He looked as if he would have a heart attack before they had gone more than a hundred yards. Joggers and bikers passed them, turning their heads for a second look at the giant bumbler and tiny toe-tapper. Some of them laughed aloud at the strange sight.

"I don't think this is working," Sierra said, yanking Brutus to a halt and catching her breath. "Maybe we should carry Peanut."

"I wish we had brought roller blades," Amy said. "Brutus could have pulled both of us with no effort. Come here, Peanut. I'll carry you."

"Why don't we put him in my backpack?" Sierra suggested. "Here, hold this." She handed Amy Brutus's leash and took off her backpack, opening the top to make room for Peanut. Scooping up the little guy, she could feel his heart pounding.

"No, come back!" Amy screamed. The leash had slipped from her hand, and Brutus had bolted toward the fountain.

"Get him!" Sierra called, quickly stuffing Peanut into her backpack and looping the straps over her shoulders. She took off running and caught up with Amy at the fountain. Brutus had dashed into the center and was lapping at the water, standing on dry ground. The fountain, for some reason, was off.

"Well, that's a good thing," Sierra said, catching her breath. "Do they turn it off like that all the time?"

"Come here, Brutus," Amy said, patting her legs and whistling. "Come, boy." She turned to Sierra for only an instant to say, "The fountain turns off like this before it changes to the next water pattern. It's going to blast any second now."

"Brutus, get over here!" Sierra yelled.

Not willing to risk getting soaked when the fountain turned back on, both girls called, whistled, and clapped their hands. No use. Brutus found the refreshing drink, as well as all the attention, to his liking. There he stood, in the center of the fountain, as all the holes in the ground began to gurgle.

KETUSH! A dozen sprays of water shot like rockets directly under Brutus, nearly lifting him on impact.

"Look at that St. Bernard. What a chump!" Sierra heard a guy behind her say. Before she could see who was insulting her dog, the same voice said, "Sierra? Amy?"

Sierra turned to see Randy, his head tilted to the side, his straight, blond hair hanging with a crooked part down the middle. He had a skateboard under his arm and was flanked by a shorter guy whom Sierra didn't know. "What are you two doing here?"

"Trying to get my dog out of the water. Come here, Brutus!"

Randy and the other guy joined the chorus, all calling Brutus out of the wet. Brutus had found a happy position, away from any direct shot of water but under an umbrella of mist.

Sierra shook her head. "It's hopeless," she said to no one in particular.

Peanut began to yip from the pack on Sierra's back. "Oh, and now I suppose you want to join him."

"What are you hiding in there?" Randy asked, stepping over and lifting the flap of Sierra's backpack. "Whoa!" he said in surprise as Peanut popped his head up and yipped in Randy's face. "Check it out, Dan. A big mouse."

"That's my dog," Amy said.

"That's a dog?" Dan asked.

"Come here, Peanut," Amy said in a cooing voice, lifting the quivering little animal from his nest. "Don't pay any attention to these mean ol' boys."

The four of them were standing with their backs to the fountain when Brutus decided to leave his invigorating shower and join them. Before Sierra could warn the others, he let loose with a mighty shake, dousing them all.

"Brutus!" Sierra reached for his collar and tried to pull the wet blob away from them. "Sorry, you guys."

"Hey, no problem. I needed a shower," Randy said. Then catching Sierra's eye, he asked, "When do you work this week?"

"Today, next Tuesday, and next Thursday." She looked at Dan and then at Randy. "Why?"

"Just wondering."

Brutus gave one last good shake before Sierra firmly gripped his leash. "You're not making this very easy on me, Brutus. You think you could try to mellow out for a few minutes?"

For an answer, Brutus let out a mighty "ruff" and bolted for the fountain, taking Sierra along with him. She didn't even have time to yell at her wayward dog. Slipping on the wet cement, she was pulled involuntarily on her backside into the fountain, where she was thoroughly soaked in two seconds.

She expected to hear a burst of laughter from the others. Instead, Randy gave a war whoop. "Water war!" he yelled, leading the way into the fountain. Dan, Amy, and Peanut all followed, hooting and hollering—and barking, in Peanut's case. For a full five minutes, Sierra and Brutus were the focus of a frenzied splash attack. Everyone was laughing and getting soaked to the skin as Brutus barked and barked.

Then the water stopped, preparing to launch a new pattern into the air. The group took advantage of the break and stepped away from the gurgling holes. They laughed and tossed meaningless threats at each other, trying to shake themselves off. A breeze swept off the Willamette River, and Sierra began to shiver.

"I'm freezing," Amy said. Her dark hair hung in her face, and she held the quivering Peanut in her arms. "We're going to the car. Bye, you guys. See you later." Amy took off at a fast trot.

"I'll be right there," Sierra said and then turned to Randy. "Why did you ask about when I worked?" She was dripping wet, but her curiosity overruled her desire to run to the warm car. She had had one casual date with Randy several weeks ago. He had promised then to take her to the movies sometime. Sierra was stubborn enough to hold him to that promise, but something in her wanted him to be the one to bring up the subject.

"I'll probably stop by to see you," Randy said. Then, lowering his voice, he added, "I want to ask you something."

"So ask me now," Sierra challenged. Her teeth were chattering.

"No, you're freezing," he said. "I'll catch you at work, okay?"

Sierra gave him a look of pretend annoyance before surrendering to the chill and the persistent yank of Brutus's leash. Then, using one of Randy's favorite words back on him, she said, "Whatever," and jogged to the car with Brutus.

She hoped she hadn't appeared too disinterested. She liked Randy, but she wasn't dazzled by him. He was a buddy—that was all.

Amy had the heater on, waiting for her. "Well? Did he ask you out?"

"No, but he said he would see me at work. And that could mean anything."

"We both know what we hope it means," Amy said, popping the gear shift into reverse. "And don't worry, I won't say anything to Vicki."

"There's nothing to say," Sierra said, rolling down her window halfway. "Phew! Does it smell like stinky, slobby dog in here or what? Brutus, you need a bath."

He let out a happy "ruff," as if he fancied the thought of more water.

## chapter two

W HEN SIERRA REACHED HOME, SHE GRABBED AN old towel from the garage and dried Brutus off before leading him to his doghouse. She entered the kitchen by the back door and found her mom standing over the stove, scrambling eggs in a large frying pan.

A slim, energetic woman, Sharon Jensen managed to keep up with her six children, and nothing usually surprised her. However, when she turned to look at Sierra, her mouth dropped slightly and she said, "What happened to you? Or do I want to know?"

"Amy and I learned that the next time we go for a morning walk, we leave the dogs at home. Brutus dragged me into the fountain." Sierra grabbed her soggy hair and held it up in a ponytail as she leaned over the warm stove. "Those eggs smell good. Can you throw in a couple more for me? I'm going to take a quick shower to get warmed up."

"They'll be ready when you are," Mom said.

A fast 10 minutes later, Sierra returned wearing her

favorite ragged overalls. Her hair was wrapped in a bath towel, twisted on top of her head. She found a plate of eggs and toast waiting for her on the kitchen counter.

Her older sister, Tawni, was sitting on a stool, sipping grapefruit juice and showing Mom her little finger on her left hand. "It got caught on the edge of the cash drawer and ripped the nail right off." Tawni worked at Nordstrom, selling perfume. At eighteen and a half, she seemed to have her life neatly in order, the same way she kept her side of the bedroom she shared with Sierra. Tawni was tall, slim, and poised, and she would never spend her Saturday morning running in a fountain the way Sierra just had with her new friends.

Mom made a sympathetic face over the broken nail.

"Do we have any honey?" Sierra asked. Mom reached into the cupboard above the dishwasher and lifted down a ceramic honey pot in the shape of a beehive.

"Did Dad tell you?" Tawni asked, turning her attention to Sierra. Tawni was dressed for work, with every hair in place. The two sisters could not look more opposite than they did at this moment.

"Tell me what?"

"About next week."

"What about next week?" Sierra said, taking a bite of eggs.

"I'm going to California with you."

"What?!" Sierra nearly choked. "Whose idea was that?"

Tawni looked surprised and then hurt. "It was your

idea, Sierra. You asked if I wanted to come with you, and I said I'd let you know."

"But that was weeks ago," Sierra said, remembering her moment of weakness when she had felt compassion for Tawni. The two of them had been in the midst of a rare civil conversation. They had agreed it had been hard for both of them to make new friends since the move to Portland.

Tawni's posture and facial expression turned to mush. "I thought you meant it," she said. "I asked Dad to look into airline tickets, and he has me booked on the flight with you. I suppose he could cancel it if you don't want me to go."

"It's just that . . ." Sierra didn't know how to say what she really felt—that she was going to visit her special friends and that they were a part of her life that had nothing to do with Tawni. Sierra didn't want to compete with her sister over her Southern California friends as she had had to compete her entire life with the perfect Tawni. "I guess I thought you didn't want to come."

"I didn't know if I wanted to or not. Then I started to think about it, and it seemed like a fun idea. It was easy to get the time off from work." Tawni stood and carried her empty glass to the sink. "But I won't come if you don't want me to."

Sierra felt her jaw clenching. She knew her mom was patiently observing, letting the two of them work things out, the way Mom always did.

"Tawni—" Sierra sucked in a nerve-replenishing

breath. "I don't mind if you come. I was surprised, that's all."

A smile returned to Tawni's face, lighting up her blue eyes. "You really don't mind?"

"No." Sierra felt fairly sure she was telling the truth.

"Great! I haven't been anywhere in so long. Tell me what we're going to do so I know what to pack."

Sierra had a sickening feeling in the pit of her stomach. "Well, we're staying at the beach with Christy's aunt and uncle. Maybe I should call and make sure they don't mind another guest."

"I thought you said it was okay for me to come."

"I didn't exactly ask Christy before I asked you."

"Oh, great! Maybe you should call her before we make any more plans."

The phrase "before we make any more plans" hit Sierra like a renegade volleyball in gym class. *We? They used to be just my plans.* "Fine. I'll call her as soon as I finish eating." At least she could keep control over eating her meal, even though her appetite had disappeared.

"Perfect," Tawni said. "I really appreciate this, Sierra. Well, I'm off. See you after five."

Sierra caught her mom's smile and nod of approval. She knew Mom thought she had handled the situation well. Too bad she didn't feel the same way. Now she had to call Christy and explain that her sister was coming. The odd part was that Christy, Katie, and Tracy were all Tawni's age—or older. Yet when Sierra roomed with these girls in England, she had felt more on their level than she did with any of her friends at home or with Tawni, who had never treated Sierra as an equal the way Christy and the others had.

Sierra put off the dreaded call all weekend. Her excuse to Tawni was she had to work from 10:00 to 4:00 at Mama Bear's, and then there was church and homework and—poof—the weekend was over.

By Tuesday evening, Sierra was still stalling. She walked in the front door as Mom stepped out of the kitchen carrying a tray with a plate of steaming vegetables, turkey, and applesauce. "Oh, good, you're home. How was work?"

Sierra knew this wasn't the time to launch into a big story about how Randy had said on Saturday morning that he would stop by work; yet he didn't come in on Saturday, he didn't talk to her at school the last two days, and he didn't come into the bakery this afternoon. Thursday was the last day she worked before her big trip to Southern California. Just when was Randy planning to stop by?

It wasn't that Mom wouldn't understand Sierra's boy problems. But at the moment, she was standing there, holding a tray of hot food in her hands. So Sierra answered with a simple "Fine."

"Good. Dinner's ready if you want to go sit down."

"Why don't I take that up to Granna Mae?" Sierra asked.

Mom looked as if she relaxed a bit. "Sure. And could you tell Tawni to come down?"

"Okay." Sierra took the dinner tray and headed up the stairs. She stopped by her bedroom first and called through the closed door, "Tawni, dinner's ready. Tell them to go ahead. I'm going to sit with Granna Mae while she eats."

Tawni opened the bedroom door and said, "Did you call your friend yet?"

"I didn't exactly have time," Sierra snapped. "I just walked in the door."

"You had better call her tonight. You're not being fair to me. I need to know, Sierra!"

"You're right, you're right. I'll call her after dinner."

Tawni swished past Sierra and headed down the stairs, an invisible trail of gardenia scent wafting in her wake, the remains of her day at work.

Sierra carefully balanced the tray and tapped on the bedroom door at the end of the hall. "It's me, Granna Mae. I brought your dinner."

"Do come in, Lovey," a high, twittery voice called.

Twisting the old doorknob, Sierra entered the large bedroom of her grandmother, who was recovering from surgery. Granna Mae was wearing her favorite white cotton nightgown with a stand-up lace collar. And to Sierra's amazement, the collar wasn't the only thing standing up.

"Granna Mae!" Sierra quickly set down the tray and rushed over to where the tottering woman with a cast on her foot stood on the soft cushion of her built-in window seat. Her arm was extended over her head.

"What are you doing?"

"I decided I had watched that spider in her web long enough!" She showed Sierra the wad of silky thread stuck to one of her lacy handkerchiefs.

"I was about to name her Charlotte. Wasn't that the spider's name in that sweet children's book?"

Sierra took the hanky and placed it on the dresser. She reached for her grandmother's elbow and helped her down. "You shouldn't be doing things like that. Tell me or Mom or Dad, and we'll come kill your spiders for you. You shouldn't be climbing on the furniture. Come back to bed."

"Oh, really now!" Granna Mae swatted the air with her hand. Taking Sierra's outstretched arm, she limped back to her bed. "I've become quite tired of all this bed rest. Do you know what I'd really like? A walk to Eaton's Pharmacy for a chocolate malt. Yes, that's what I fancy for my dinner this evening. A look at the last tulips of spring around the neighborhood and a visit with my friends at Eaton's. You can take me there, can't you, Lovey?"

Granna Mae had broken her foot when she was in the hospital for emergency gall bladder surgery. She had decided to go for a little walk one evening, pulled out her IV, and then fell in the hospital gift shop. In recent years, Granna Mae's mind had begun to play tricks on her, so Sierra's family had moved here from a small town near Lake Tahoe, California, to live with her in her old Victorian home. Whenever she was thinking clearly, Granna Mae called Sierra "Lovey."

"I'll ask Dad," Sierra said. "First you need to eat your dinner before it gets cold." She held back the covers so Granna Mae could slip into bed.

"What did you bring me?" Granna Mae asked, slowly hoisting her legs under the covers. She leaned forward while Sierra adjusted the pillows behind her grand-mother's back and tucked the blanket around her. With her hands folded on top of the handmade patchwork quilt, she looked at Sierra expectantly—innocently.

"Turkey, Granna Mae. Are you hungry?"

"Yes, I am, and turkey suits me fine. Are you going to eat with me?"

"No, but I'll stay with you."

Granna Mae reached over and slipped her cool hand into Sierra's. It felt like wrinkled silk, soft and familiar. "And you'll pray with me, won't you?"

"Of course." Sierra bowed her head and closed her eyes, allowing her ruffled emotions to settle down. She loved being with her dear grandmother alone like this and praying with her. With four brothers and one sister, Sierra had had little time alone with her grandmother when Sierra was growing up. But every time her family visited through the years, Granna Mae had always found a way, found the time, to sit down with each of the grandchildren and pray with him or her. It always made Sierra feel special and singled out from the bunch. Sierra grew up believing that's how God thought of her, too—as one-of-a-kind and worthy of His love and attention.

"Amen," Granna Mae said when Sierra finished

praying. She squeezed Sierra's hand. "Now, tell me all about your day. How did you do on your science test?"

"That was yesterday. I did fine."

"Another A, I suspect," Granna Mae said, cutting her turkey with slightly quivering hands.

"I think so."

"Don't ever take those brains of yours for granted, Lovey. Do you hear me?"

Sierra nodded and smiled. Learning came easily to her. She still had to study to get A's, but it was never hard. The hardest part was feeling motivated enough to care about whether she was getting straight A's or not. Grades didn't matter that much to Sierra.

"And when do you leave for your great adventure in England?"

"I already went to England. That was last January, remember? I'm going down to Southern California on Friday to see the friends I met in England."

"Oh, yes." Granna Mae slipped a dainty spoonful of vegetables into her mouth and nodded at Sierra. She swallowed and asked, "And will Paul be there?"

Sierra quietly bit the inside of her lower lip. She had an uncle named Paul who had been killed in Vietnam. Often when Granna Mae's memory turned fuzzy, she would ask about Paul.

"Ah, no. My friends down there are Christy, Katie, Tracy, Doug, and Todd."

Granna Mae reached for the china cup that held her strong, black coffee, and she took a sip. "Pity that you won't see that nice Paul. You know he brought me daffys at the hospital and kept me company for hours my last night there. He is such a dear young man."

Now Sierra knew her grandmother hadn't slipped into another time zone. She was talking about a different Paul. This Paul was the one Sierra had met at the airport in England. Their relationship, if one could call it that, was a strange blending of chance meetings and a few pithy letters. That was all.

"No, Granna Mae, Paul won't be there."

"Pity," she repeated, stirring the applesauce.

Sierra had settled in the overstuffed chair by the fireplace, slipped off her shoes, and curled her legs underneath her to keep her bare feet warm. She hadn't allowed herself the luxury of thinking about Paul for quite a few days, maybe even weeks. They had experienced such an intense connection when they had first met. Her grandmother almost sounded as if she had a strong affection for him, too. Why was that?

"You must pray for that young man," Granna Mae said. "Do you?"

"I did for a while, but . . ."

There was a quick tap on the door. Tawni opened it and said, "Sierra, you have a phone call. I think it's Christy."

# chapter three

"**A**RE YOU SURE YOUR AUNT AND UNCLE WON'T mind?" Sierra asked Christy on the phone down in her dad's study. She had retreated there to have some privacy. It was her favorite room in the house, and she was sitting in her favorite chair.

"No, I'm sure they won't," Christy said. "My uncle likes having us around, and my aunt likes to . . ." She seemed to search for the right word. "She likes planning things. I'm sure she'll like you and your sister. Tell me your flight time again so I can write it down."

Sierra repeated the information, and Christy said, "One of us will pick you up at the airport and drive you to Newport Beach. If Katie and I can't get up there soon enough, Todd said he would pick you up. Then we'll meet at my aunt and uncle's house. I'm sure they're planning on having dinner with us that night. The next day is open. We can hang out at the beach or go shopping or whatever you want."

"You guys don't have to entertain us," Sierra said. "We don't have to go anywhere. The beach is enough for me."

"Todd and Doug are bringing a bunch of their friends from the San Diego God Lovers' group."

"Sounds fun."

"I'm sure it will be. I'm really glad you're coming. Our time together in England went so fast. Makes me wish you lived down here."

"I know. Me, too. Thanks for inviting me, and I appreciate your letting Tawni come, too."

"Sure. You and Tawni must be pretty close."

Sierra tilted her head toward the phone receiver. The door to her dad's study was open, and she didn't know who might be able to hear her. "Not really. This was her idea, not mine."

"I'm sure it'll be fine," Christy said reassuringly. "The guest room is plenty big for the four of us—you, me, Katie, and Tawni. And there'll be so many people around all week. I'm sure Tawni will have a good time, and you will, too. It'll be like a big reunion all week. I can't wait!"

"I'm looking forward to it," Sierra said. "I hope I didn't sound negative about my sister. It's just that I guess it would have been easier or different or something if I were coming by myself." Then, changing the subject, she said, "How's Todd doing?"

"Great as always."

Sierra thought she heard a smile in Christy's voice. "Did he decide about going back to Spain?"

"Not yet. Lots of factors need to be considered. He's taking classes at the University of California, Irvine, this semester. I think I told you that before. And he's been in communication with the missions director at Carnforth Hall. They'll gladly take him on staff in Spain or anywhere in Europe when he wants to make the commitment."

"And where does that leave you?"

"I'm taking 17 units this semester at the community college. I want to get my AA degree in early childhood development as soon as possible. After that, it's up to God."

"You and Todd haven't made any plans?"

"No. If one theme runs through our relationship, it's s-l-o-w. Everything has gone slowly for us, and just because we're both on the same side of the globe now, that hasn't changed. I don't mind, though. For now it feels just right. How about you? Whatever happened with that guy you met at the airport?"

"Paul? Nothing."

"Then what about the guy from your school who came over? Was it Randy? Did he ever take you out again?"

"No," Sierra said with a sigh. "Until this weekend, he had been ignoring me. Then he said he would come see me at work, but he hasn't; and today he practically ignored me again."

"Sounds like an average guy to me," Christy said. "Don't get discouraged. Who knows? You might meet someone here next week. One of Doug's friends maybe. Newport Beach is a wonderful place to meet someone special."

"I take it that's where you met Todd."

"Yep. Almost five years ago. Can you believe it?"

"Five years! You and Todd should be the poster couple for the 'Love Waits' campaign."

Christy laughed. "It doesn't seem that long. A lot has happened during those five years. But I do agree that true love is worth the wait. I'd wait another five years for Todd if I had to. He's the only man for me. Ever."

An hour after hanging up from her call with Christy, Sierra still felt a warm glow. There was something encouraging and beautiful about two people who were in love the way Christy and Todd were. It made Sierra wonder if she would be willing to wait 10 years to marry a guy if she were so intensely in love with him. Maybe it was good that she had never had a boyfriend. Being in love at 16 could create all kinds of problems.

The next evening the thought surfaced again in Sierra's mind while she was doing her homework. She asked Tawni if she felt ready to marry. Tawni stood over her open luggage, meticulously folding the pile of T-shirts she had laid on her bed alongside a pile of jeans, shorts, and enough accessories to open a jewelry stand at a swap meet.

"Am I ready to marry? Why are you asking me such a pointless question? I'm not even dating anyone."

"I know, but if you met someone and fell in love, would you want to marry him now, or would you wait?"

"Wait for what?"

"Oh, never mind," Sierra said, returning to her homework.

"When do you plan to pack, Sierra?"

"Tomorrow."

"Are all your clothes clean? Wait. That was a ridiculous question. Of course your clothes aren't clean. I want you to know that I'm not going to help you pull your stuff together at the last minute, and I don't want you to plan on borrowing any of my clothes once we get down there."

"Like I would," Sierra said. Even though she and Tawni were about the same size, their tastes were opposite. Sierra's style was carefree and casual. Tawni preferred color-coordinated, classic-style clothes.

A knock at their door was followed by their dad's clean-shaven face peeking in. "The boys and I are taking Granna Mae for a little ride down to Eaton's. You girls want to come? Shakes are on me."

"No."

"No thanks, Dad. I have too much homework," Sierra said.

"And she needs to wash her clothes for next week," Tawni added.

"Sure you can't take a break?" he asked, stepping into the room. Howard Jensen was a trim man with a receding hairline and a perpetually "open" look about him, which made him seem approachable any time, regarding any subject. He had a way of making Sierra feel as if she were his only child, not one of six. She suspected the others felt the same way. "Free chocolate shakes," he said, trying to tempt them.

"I better keep at this," Sierra said, nodding toward the books surrounding her where she sat in bed, knees up, pillow against the headboard and notebook open in her elevated lap. "I'm glad you're taking Granna Mae. She'll be happy."

"I never need to be asked twice when it comes to having a malt at Eaton's. Should we bring something back for either of you?"

"Not for me," Sierra said.

"You know I'm on a diet, Dad," Tawni said.

"Right. I forgot." He ducked out, and a couple minutes later they heard him call into Granna Mae's room, "Your carriage awaits you, madam."

The sound of shuffling feet followed and then the echoing calls of their younger brothers, Gavin and Dillon, at the bottom of the stairs asking if they could take Brutus with them.

"As long as he's on a leash," Dad called back.

Sierra smiled. As if a leash made a difference with that walrus. She wanted to join them. It would be so much easier to forget all this homework and go have some fun. Plenty of light remained in the dusky sky this mild spring night. The endless Portland rains had let up for the past few days, and a warm, sweet scent filled the air. Sierra reminded herself that in a few days she would be having plenty of fun on a sunny beach in Southern California. For now, she had work to do.

"Do you think I should take both my bathing suits?" Tawni asked.

"Sure. Why not? They don't take up much room," Sierra said. "I'm taking all three of mine."

"I can't decide," Tawni said.

"Take both of them. Because once we get there, you're not borrowing any of my clothes!" Sierra playfully pointed her pencil at Tawni and shook it to emphasize her words.

"Like I would," Tawni muttered, placing both bathing suits inside her suitcase.

*chapter four*

Thursday afternoon Sierra arrived at Mama Bear's a few minutes early and entered through the back door. She found her blue apron waiting, along with a pan of Mama Bear's famous cinnamon rolls on the lunch table. This is where they put the rolls jokingly referred to as the "burnt sacrifices" of the day. At least one pan a day was deemed unfit to sell by the owner, Mrs. Kraus, which left the employees free to eat to their hearts' content. Sierra pulled off a big piece. It was still warm—the only way to enjoy a Mama Bear's cinnamon roll.

"Hi, Sierra," Jody called to her from the front register. "I'm glad you're here. I have to leave early to run to the bank. Are you ready to take over?"

Sierra couldn't answer with the sticky wad in her mouth. She made her way to the front, tying her apron as she went and massaging the roll in her mouth. She faced Jody and nodded, still not able to swallow the bite.

"Good grief, girl," her fellow employee said. "A whole pan is back there. You don't have to down it all in one bite!"

Sierra quickly swallowed and joined Jody in a laugh.

"Okay. I'm all set now. You can go."

"You sure?"

Sierra nodded.

"I like you," Jody said. "Did I ever tell you that?"

Sierra thought, *Just every time I work the same days you do.* She smiled her mutual appreciation back to Jody and poured herself a cup of water.

"You add spunk to this place," Jody said, untying her apron. "I'm going to miss you next week."

"I'll bring you back some sand from the beach," Sierra said.

"No, don't. It'll only make me jealous. And don't you dare come back all tanned, with your hair bleached white."

"I promise my hair won't be bleached white, but I can't promise about the tan. That's one of the hazards, you know, of lounging on the beach all day for a week."

"Oh, hush. I don't want to hear about it. I'm leaving," Jody said, exiting with a friendly wave. She was in her early thirties and was the divorced mother of two. She worked two jobs and never seemed to have enough time to run errands. More than once Sierra had covered for her so she could drive her kids to the dentist or soccer practice. Sierra and Jody rarely worked the same hours.

The shop was quiet this afternoon, as usual for this time of day. Three women sat at a table by the window, bent forward in solemn conversation. Two men in business suits looked together at the screen of a laptop computer. Sierra noticed they both had coffee and went over with the fresh pot and offered them refills. She did the same for the women.

Then the door opened, and Randy stepped in, his crooked smile lighting up his face.

Sierra held up the coffeepot and, playing out the waitress role, said, "Coffee, sir?"

She tried to mask that she was irritated at him for being so mysterious. First, on Saturday he had said he would come see her. Then he pretty much avoided her all week at school. Now, here he was showing up on Thursday, as if this were what he meant all along. If he hadn't been so shy and inexperienced at dating, she would have been mad at him.

"Got milk?" Randy answered. "And the biggest cinnamon roll in the house. With extra frosting."

"Coming right up," Sierra said, returning to the area behind the counter. Randy followed her and leaned against the glass bakery case as she served his cinnamon roll and milk.

"Any chance you can take a break and sit down with me?" he asked.

"Not right now. I'm the only one here except for Andy in the back. I need to stay behind the counter."

"Then I'll eat right here." He handed her some money and popped open the top of the milk carton, slugging it down all at once. "Better get me another milk," he said. "And a cup of water, if you don't mind, miss."

"Not a bit." Sierra felt a flock of flapping butterflies

begin a dance inside her stomach. Why should she feel nervous? She handed him the change and set another carton of milk and a cup of ice water on the counter for him. He was already two bites into the cinnamon roll.

"Good, aren't they?"

Now Randy was the one with the gooey ball of dough in his mouth, and he could only nod his agreement.

*So, come on, Randy, what's the big mysterious thing you wanted to ask me?* she thought. *It took you long enough to finally come in. Are you going to ask me out or not?*

Finally, he said, "What kind of flowers do you like?"

"Me?" It was the last question in the world Sierra expected him to ask.

He nodded and took another bite of his cinnamon roll. The white frosting dripped down the corner of his mouth.

Sierra motioned with her finger on the side of her mouth. Randy caught the hint and reached for a napkin. Another customer entered the store, setting off the cheery bell over the front door. At the sound, Randy stepped aside so the woman could order a box of cinnamon rolls to go. Then another customer came in who wanted a cappuccino. Sierra went through the familiar motions of preparing the specialty coffee drink and making change for the man's $20 bill. By the time she was ready to answer Randy's question, he had finished his snack and was casually waiting for her with his arm across the top of the cash register.

"You wanted to know what kind of flowers I like?" she

said. In the several minutes that had passed since he had asked, her mind had run through every possible reason Randy would pose such a question. All her hopes pointed to the obvious—and very flattering—conclusion.

"Right. What kind do you like?"

"That would depend. What would the flowers be for?"

"A corsage."

"And what would the corsage be for?"

"A spring benefit for the Portland Center for the Performing Arts. Two weeks from tomorrow night at the downtown Hilton."

Sierra thought this had to be the most backward way a guy had ever asked a girl out in the history of the world. But Randy was creative—and a little shy. This seemed to fit his style. She remembered that his father had been in a band. Perhaps this was a yearly event Randy attended with his family. She immediately started to think about what she would wear to such a formal event.

"Roses are always nice. Or carnations. But carnations can be kind of bulky and heavy on a dress. Let's see, orchids make me think of an old lady. I'd say rosebuds. A soft color like yellow or pink. Oh, I know—have you ever seen those peach-colored tea roses? Those would be really pretty in a corsage."

"Peach-colored tea roses. Okay."

Sierra smiled her anticipation at Randy. She had never been given flowers before, or asked to a formal anything. It would be fun to go to something like this with Randy since he was so easygoing and such a sincere friend. She wondered if she would have time to find a dress during the week after Easter vacation. Or maybe they could go shopping in California, as Christy had suggested. It couldn't be too fancy; yet it would have to be nice enough so that the tea rose corsage wouldn't look out of place. Tawni would certainly volunteer to do her makeup. And her parents would want to take pictures.

Sierra's imagination continued to sprint through all the details as another customer stepped into the shop and ordered a single roll to go.

After she handed the customer the white bag and his change, Randy glanced at his watch.

"I have to run. Hey, do me a favor and don't say anything about this to Vicki, okay?"

"Sure." Sierra wasn't sure why he would say such a thing except maybe Vicki was beginning to be interested in Randy, and he didn't want her to be jealous of Sierra. "See you tomorrow at school."

"See you," he echoed, and he was out the door.

Sierra began her afternoon cleanup chores, starting with wiping down the counters. *Two weeks from tomorrow night*, she repeated to herself. *Maybe I can find a black dress and wear my ivory lace vest. Or something from the vintage shop in a sheer fabric with a full skirt. I should have told him white roses. White flowers would be easier to match than peach. Why did I ever tell him peach?*

A few more customers found their way into the shop during the next hour and a half. A few minutes before closing, the door opened, and Sierra looked up to see that her last customer of the day was her mom.

"Hi, honey." Mom wore jogging clothes, and her blond hair was pulled back in what Tawni called a nub of a ponytail. Tawni's hair was long and silky and hung past her shoulders, where it curled naturally on the ends. Tawni had little sympathy for Sierra's wild mane or Mom's thin, straight hair, which took a fair amount of effort to work into a presentable style. "I thought you might like some company on your walk home."

"Wait till you hear my news!" Sierra said, locking up the cash register and putting her apron in the back. She said good night to Andy and left the shop, her arm linked in her mom's.

"Randy came in, and he asked me out to a formal dinner two weeks from tomorrow! It's a benefit for the music center downtown or something. He asked what kind of flowers I liked, and guess what I told him?"

"I can't imagine," her mom said as they marched up the street toward home.

"Peach-colored tea roses. Where in the world did I come up with that?"

"I don't know. And what are you going to wear?"

"I think I need something new."

"Do you mean new, new? Or new to you, from a thrift store?"

"Either. Whatever. Something nice. I know I shouldn't be so excited since it's just Randy," Sierra confessed, "but this is really fun! I can't believe he asked me."

"I can." She gave Sierra's arm a squeeze. "You just wait,

Sierra Mae Jensen. Once the word is out, there will be standing room only as the eligible young men of Portland line up, waiting to ask you out."

"Yeah," Sierra said dryly, "don't I wish."

Sierra imagined what that line would look like. There would be half a dozen surfer-type guys from Christy's beach crowd, a few guys from school, including Randy at the front of the line, and way at the back would be a lone figure in a brown leather jacket, wearing an Indiana Jones–style hat, just like the one Paul had on when she met him.

It was only a dream, but an intriguing one, and one Sierra decided to carry around with her for a while.

## chapter five

FRIDAY AT SCHOOL, ALL SIERRA HAD WERE HER dreams—her dreams and a headache. She had stayed up late, packing for the trip, much to Tawni's disgust, and Randy said only five words to her the whole day: "Bye. Have a nice vacation."

Everyone was a bit frenzied, though, turning in reports and homework before the week off. Sierra planned to tell Amy about Randy coming to Mama Bear's and asking her out, but there was never a convenient moment when they were far enough away from listening ears.

Mom and Tawni picked Sierra up from school the minute classes were dismissed. They drove to the airport in less than 20 minutes and parked the car so Mom could walk in to see them off. Everything went as smooth as could be, and 45 minutes later, Sierra and Tawni were in the air, winging their way south.

"Look how green everything is," Tawni said from her window seat. "I got tired of the rain this winter, but when you see the results from this view, it seems worth it."

Sierra didn't answer. She was lost in a memory of her

flight home from England when she had sat next to Paul and they had discussed life. She had been her usual blunt self, which hadn't scared Paul. Her relationship with Randy was different. She didn't feel as if she had to prove anything with him—but then again, it didn't matter as much if he liked her or not.

Christy's words from the other day returned to her, and Sierra thought about what it would be like if she met someone this week. Long walks on the beach. Shared jokes and goofing off with her friends. Good-byes and promises to write. Mom had always encouraged her to dream, and dream she did. Only, none of her dreams for this week included Tawni.

They exited the plane right on time, and Sierra began to scan the faces at the crowded airport.

"Which of your friends has the red hair?" Tawni asked.

"Katie. Christy's hair is more like yours. Long, brown, and sort of straight."

"My hair isn't straight."

"Okay, long, brown, and sort of whatever."

"They're not here," Tawni said, looking around. "This is just great, Sierra. What are we going to do now?"

"Relax, will you? She said they would be here. Keep looking."

They stood together in the middle of the walkway, Sierra clutching her backpack and Tawni holding her vanity kit with both hands. Harried travelers brushed past them, and the noise of the terminal began to close in on Sierra.

"I could call her," Sierra suggested.

"I think you had better."

"But if she's on her way here, or stuck in traffic, she won't be home."

"Someone might be there who can tell you what's going on. We're making a spectacle of ourselves, standing here like this."

"Okay, okay," Sierra conceded, opening her backpack and looking for her address book.

Over the clamor of the airport crowds, Sierra heard a loud, "Hey, Sierra! Over here."

They both looked and saw a tall, blond surfer dodging his way toward them. As he neared, Sierra noticed his screaming silver-blue eyes.

"Todd!" Sierra opened her arms to receive his breathless hug. The back of his T-shirt was wet with perspiration.

"How's it going? Hey, Tawni," he said, turning to Sierra's surprised yet obviously impressed sister. He gave her a quick, welcoming hug and said, "I'm Todd."

"Hello," Tawni said, all her best manners and posture coming to the fore. "It's nice to meet you."

"Let me carry that for you," he said, reaching for Tawni's makeup case. Sierra had teased Tawni about it, saying it looked like a little girl's play suitcase and should have the words "Going to Grandma's" printed across the side.

"That's okay," Tawni said, unwilling to surrender the case. "I've got it."

"I take it you have more luggage, though."

"Slightly," Sierra said with a laugh. "Which way to the baggage claim area?"

"Follow me. Christy should be at Bob and Marti's by the time we get there. She was running too late with the Friday afternoon traffic; so she called and asked me to pick you up. Sorry to keep you waiting."

"Oh, don't worry about it," Tawni said, stepping next to Todd. "We didn't wait long. We really appreciate your going out of your way like this. Thanks."

"No problem."

They entered the baggage claim area, and Sierra reached for Tawni, pulling her back by the elbow. "He's taken," Sierra whispered, making a face.

Tawni made a face back. A cloud of dread moved in and hung over Sierra's head. What if her sister went after Todd in a big way this week, and what if Todd fell for her charms? Tawni was, by far, more gorgeous than Christy, more refined, and much more aggressive. Was it possible that Sierra would be responsible for assisting in the breakup of Todd and Christy by introducing her sister to him? The thought was too horrible to dwell on. She walked to the edge of the moving carousel and reached for her bag as it came around.

Behind her, she could hear Tawni's silky voice questioning Todd. "So, this is your senior year in college? Then what do you plan to do?"

"Not sure yet," Todd said.

"I have mine," Sierra said, breaking into their conversation and dropping her bag on the ground. "How many did you have, Tawni?"

"Only three," she answered with a veiled dark look at Sierra.

"I'll help you," Todd offered.

"Oh, would you? Thanks." Tawni's smile at Todd was warmer than any Sierra had ever seen on her sister's face.

*Oh brother!* Sierra thought. *So this is how my nightmare begins. Christy is never going to forgive me for bringing Tawni.*

They waited until the last piece of luggage had come through the opening and the carousel had stopped moving. They stood there for a few minutes more, expecting the conveyor belt to kick back on and pump out Tawni's three bags. It never did.

"This is awful," Tawni said. "Nothing like this has ever happened to me."

"Come on," Todd said, leading them to a service representative at a nearby counter and explaining the situation. After nearly an hour, Todd finally convinced Tawni that all they could do was fill out the forms and leave Bob and Marti's address. The airport would deliver the missing luggage once it showed up.

"I can't believe this," Tawni said, clutching her makeup kit even tighter. "I'll have to go shopping right away."

"You can borrow some of my stuff," Sierra said sweetly, enjoying the irony of the situation. She couldn't imagine Tawni ever wearing her baggy jeans or gauze peasant skirts.

"Why don't we go to Bob and Marti's first?" Todd suggested. "You can make your plans from there."

Tawni was silent as they walked to the parking lot. Todd led them to a Mercedes and unlocked it with a security pad on his key chain. The expression Tawni flashed at Sierra said, "Not only is he gorgeous, he's rich, too!" Tawni slid into the front passenger seat, and Sierra, without bothering to comment, climbed into the backseat.

"Nice car," Tawni said as they pulled out of the parking place.

"Yeah, it is," Todd said.

"Have you had it long?" Sierra asked.

"It's not mine. It's Bob's. He's had this one quite a few years. My mode of transportation is undergoing a transplant this week. We're all hoping the old guy makes it through."

As they pulled out of the airport into the heavy traffic, Tawni rolled down her window and stuck out her arm. "It's sure a lot warmer here than what we left this afternoon. So tell me, Todd, what are our plans for the week?"

"You'll have to ask Christy that. I'm just along for the ride."

"Oh, I am too," Tawni said. Sierra watched from the backseat as Tawni looked over at Todd and examined his profile. "I haven't been here since I was a kid. You'll have to show me all the hot spots."

Todd didn't respond. He looked straight ahead, speeding a little to make it through a yellow light. Sierra wondered if he would have acted any differently if Tawni weren't there. Certainly not. Certainly, Todd was as in love with Christy as she obviously was with him. At least he had seemed that way in England when Sierra first met him. But then, Tawni hadn't been there to mix things up.

# chapter six

"WELCOME, WELCOME! COME ON IN." THE dark-haired, middle-aged man in a white golf shirt and shorts showed them into his impressive beachfront home. "Which one of you is Sierra?"

"Me."

"And this must be your sister."

"Tawni. I'm pleased to meet you, Mr.—" Tawni held out her hand to shake his.

"Call me Bob. Please. Come on in. How was your flight?"

"They lost my luggage," Tawni said, stepping into the wide entryway. The house was decorated in a modern motif. "You have a beautiful home."

"Save all the praise for my wife," Bob said. "She eats it up. Marti? They're here!" he called into the living room. "I think she's out on the patio with the girls."

"Christy's here?" Todd asked.

Sierra thought his expression brightened. Before Bob could answer, Todd had deserted them, taking long strides through the living room.

"Shall we join him?" Bob asked. He led the way through the living room, with its picture windows looking out onto an inviting stretch of sand and endless blue ocean beyond. Early evening sunlight flooded the area, illuminating the white furniture and white baby grand piano in the corner.

Sierra peered through the sliding glass door that opened to the cement patio facing the beach, and she saw Todd and Christy in a tight embrace. *Good,* she thought with a sense of relief. *Now Tawni will see that her efforts are wasted on this guy.*

They joined the small group on the patio, but before Bob could begin the introductions, Katie let out a squeal, hopped up from the chaise lounge, and gave Sierra a whopping hug. Christy hugged her next and then introduced her to Aunt Marti, which is where the hugging stopped cold.

The woman gave Sierra the shivers. It wasn't her appearance. She was very nice-looking—petite, trim, with dark hair and flawless makeup. She wore casual pants and a long, flowing top that looked like silk and was the color of a persimmon. She wore a lot of jewelry, all gold. "Well maintained," her dad would have called her. It seemed to Sierra an invisible wall of ice surrounded this woman. She was not at all what Sierra had expected.

"Please," Marti said, taking command of the chatter. "Sierra, Tawni, help yourselves to the beverages over there on the tray. Then do come join us."

Sierra reminded herself that this woman, no matter

how cold, was their hostess. "Thank you," Sierra said, forcing her warmest smile.

Beyond the small patio where they had gathered ran a wide sidewalk along the front of the house. The houses along this stretch of beach seemed to be built right next to each other, and almost all of them were two stories. Some homes down the way appeared older and considerably smaller in size. However, Bob and Marti's and the two next door were large, and their patios were well stocked with expensive patio furniture.

Marti showed the two sisters to the beverage cart a few feet away. Her glance rested only a moment on Sierra before landing soundly on Tawni. "Tell me, Tawni, how long have you been modeling for Nordstrom?"

"Modeling? I don't model for them. I work at a fragrance counter at one of the stores in Portland."

"No!" Marti pressed her manicured hand to her chest. "You don't do any modeling?"

Tawni's laugh sounded innocent and sincere to Sierra. "No, I don't model."

Sierra dropped several melting ice cubes into a glass and reached for a bottle of kiwi-strawberry Snapple. Tawni stood right behind her and selected a bottle of mineral water. Her choice seemed to please Marti, who said, "What a terrible waste of such a face and figure. You really should consider modeling, Tawni."

"I never thought of it."

"Oh, come now, never?"

Tawni shook her head.

"It just so happens," Marti said, "that I know a few people in the industry, and well, that is, if you would be interested, I could make a few calls on your behalf."

"Interested in what?"

"In putting together a portfolio. Meeting with an agent. Starting your modeling career. That is, if you're interested."

Tawni looked as if her fairy godmother had just arrived and showered her with wish dust. "I . . . I don't know. I never thought of it before."

"Oh, come now. I have a hard time believing that. Surely you've looked in the mirror."

Out of the corner of her eye, Sierra caught Katie making a face to Christy. Christy only pursed her lips together and swallowed whatever her true reaction was.

"If you all will kindly excuse us," Marti said, aligning herself with Tawni, "we'll be in my office for a bit." With a grand, gracious gesture, she invited Tawni back inside.

Sierra sat at one of the chairs pulled out from around the patio table. Todd and Christy were seated a few feet away on the low, cement-block wall, holding hands and looking as if they should have their picture taken.

Katie had returned to her lounge chair, and Bob sat down next to Sierra at the table.

"What was all that about?" Sierra asked.

"Well, you did it, Sierra!" Katie said with a hearty laugh. "You made Marti's wish come true! You brought her the perfect Barbie doll. Something Christy never could be, and something none of Christy's friends turned out to be."

Sierra turned to Bob, expecting him to be offended by Katie's outburst. His grin was subtle, but it was there, all right. A twinkle in his eyes tipped off Sierra that, although he would never admit it or join in the conversation, he agreed with Katie.

"I can't believe this," Sierra said, shaking her head. "What an introduction to Southern California!"

"It's only the beginning," Todd said. "We might not see too much of your sister the rest of the week."

Sierra wanted to blurt out that that would be fine with her, but she held her tongue.

"Something tells me your sister can hold her own against my aunt," Christy said. "Marti means well. It's just that she . . ."

"She needs Jesus," Todd said, filling in the blank for Christy.

"Definitely," Katie echoed.

Sierra turned to Bob and said, "It must be hard being married to a non-Christian."

There was an awkward silence. Then Bob said slowly, "That would depend. Do you mean, is it hard for me being married to Marti or for Marti being married to me, since neither of us is what you would probably classify as a Christian?"

Sierra realized she had put her foot in her mouth big time. "I didn't mean to say that," she stammered. Her cheeks turned red.

"Doesn't bother me," he said. "I firmly believe that everyone should believe in something. And right now I believe I should start the barbecue." He rose and gave Sierra a wink. "Don't worry about it," he said. "I like it when a woman learns early on to speak her mind." Then, looking over Sierra's head at Katie, he said, "That's why I like Katie so much."

"The admiration is mutual," Katie replied. "Now if you would just get saved!"

"Oh, you never know," Bob said. "The prayer of a righteous person has a powerful effect. Wasn't that our verse last week, Todd?"

Todd nodded.

"And I'd say you guys are about the most self-righteous young men and women I've ever met."

"Very funny," Katie countered.

"You want some help with the grill?" Todd asked.

"Naw. I got it. You can hold a spatula any day. What you're holding at the moment is much more important." Bob winked at Christy and then rounded the corner of the house, disappearing down the side patio, whistling to himself.

Sierra dropped her head in her hands. "This is the most bizarre first meeting I've ever experienced! Are you guys always so intensely honest? And how come he knew that verse?"

"Bob has been going to a morning Bible study with me for the past few months," Todd said.

"You're kidding. He's not a believer, but he's willing to go with you?"

"Sure. Why not? The guys treat him like an equal. He's

honestly seeking. There's no better place for him to be than with a bunch of other seekers and believers. My dad's been going, too, this past month."

"At least your dad is willing to look into Christianity," Katie said. "My parents won't even go to a Christmas service with me. They keep telling me I'll grow out of this delusion. Christy, however, has the storybook life."

"Your parents are Christians, too, aren't they, Sierra?" Christy asked.

"My whole family is. Parents, brothers, sister, grandparents. Everyone I know. I think I take it too much for granted."

"I know I do," Christy said.

Suddenly, from the side of the house came a loud whooshing sound like a gust of wind, immediately followed by frantic screams.

# chapter seven

**T**ODD BOLTED FROM THE WALL AND RAN AROUND TO the side of the house with Katie sprinting after him. Christy and Sierra remained frozen for a second as ear-piercing screams filled the air. Marti came running out to the patio with Tawni right behind her. "What happened? What's going on?"

Sierra and Christy sprang from their seats at the same moment and rounded the corner to see Todd embracing Bob in a full body hug, then dropping to the ground and rolling on the cement. Smoke rose from the two men and the beach towel Todd had stuffed between them. Reckless flames leapt three feet from the gas barbecue, lapping at the stucco wall of the garage.

Katie grabbed another beach towel, and edging her way to the grill, she reached to turn the knob.

"Katie, don't!" Christy screamed, causing Katie to momentarily withdraw her arm.

Marti arrived right behind them and began to shriek.

Katie yelled, "Call 911! Now!" Then, ducking from the flames, she turned the knob, and the fire began to decline.

49

Marti continued to shriek.

Sierra turned and ran into the house, frantically searching for a phone. She found one on the wall in the kitchen and dialed 911. Trying to think clearly and steady her breathing, she repeated to the person on the other end what had happened.

Christy dashed into the kitchen and took the phone from her, explaining the situation in greater detail and giving the address. She stayed on the line, and Sierra stood beside her, shaking, as they waited for the ambulance to arrive. The minute they heard the sirens, they ran to the front door and let in the team of paramedics and firefighters.

Everything was chaotic. Sierra couldn't watch as they loaded Bob and Todd onto stretchers. Marti had fainted, and they placed her on a stretcher as well. The firefighters checked the eaves and roof for flyaway sparks while a policeman questioned Christy and wrote down notes as she bravely tried to describe what had happened.

Katie appeared to be the least shaken of any of them. She stood still while the paramedics examined her singed eyebrows and hair. The beach towel she had wrapped around her arm lay in a sooty mound next to the now silent barbecue.

"We'd like to take you in, all the same," the paramedic said to Katie. "Just to be safe."

"You guys want to come?" Katie asked. She made it sound more like a joy ride than a trip to the hospital in an ambulance.

"I can follow you in the car," Christy said.

"Forget it," Katie said. "You need to be in there with Todd right this minute. I can drive these guys."

"We don't need to go, if it's a problem," Sierra offered.

"Tell you what," one of the paramedics said, interrupting their volley of carpooling ideas. "I'll make the decision for you. You're all coming, and you're going to ride where I tell you to ride."

Twenty minutes later, they were in the emergency room at Hoag Memorial Hospital. Tawni and Sierra found empty seats in the waiting area while Katie and Christy went in with Marti and the men. Marti had come to in the ambulance and was crying hysterically. They could hear gut-wrenching moans from Bob as he and Todd were wheeled past them.

"This is so awful," Tawni said, the tears welling up. "I can't believe this happened!"

"I think they're going to be okay," Sierra said calmly. "It looked like Todd put a towel between them, and that probably put out most of the fire."

"But did you see Bob's arm?" Tawni whispered. "His ear . . ." Her voice trailed off.

Sierra hadn't looked on purpose. The ghastly smell of burnt flesh and hair had overpowered her when she had gone back outside after the paramedics had arrived. She knew she couldn't look.

Five minutes passed before either of them spoke. "Do you think we should check on them?" Tawni asked.

"I think they'll come out and tell us," Sierra said. Over

their heads, a television blared with a rerun of "Taxi." Nothing was funny about any of it. The canned laughter made Sierra angry. Why did they have to have that stupid thing on, anyhow? Couldn't they let people sit and wait in peace?

A woman entered the emergency room with a crying baby in her arms. A nurse took her behind the double doors to the emergency area, and the infant's wail grew fainter.

"I could never work in a place like this," Sierra whispered to Tawni.

"Me either. Do you think they're okay in there?"

"I don't know. I think we should pray, Tawni."

"I have been."

"I know. I have been, too," Sierra said. "But I think we should pray together." She bowed her head, leaned closer to her sister, and started to pray before Tawni had a chance to agree or disagree. Sierra's prayer was long and sincere. When she finished, she looked up to see a guy sitting on the edge of the coffee table, head bowed, apparently praying with them. The minute she heard him begin his prayer with, "I agree, Father," she felt warm and comforted. It was Doug, her team leader from the missions trip in England.

When Doug finished, another guy, whom Sierra didn't know, began to pray. When he said, "Amen," Sierra sprang from her chair and wrapped her arms around Doug's neck, hugging him and letting the pent-up tears come out. She pulled away, looked him in the face, and gave him her best attempt at a smile. "Hi," she said in a small voice.

Doug's face usually resembled that of a boy walking around secretly hiding a frog in his pocket. At this moment, he looked more serious than Sierra had ever seen him.

"We stopped by, and the neighbors told us," Doug said. "Have you heard anything?"

"Not yet. Bob and Todd were burned. Katie got singed, and Marti fainted."

"Sounds about right for Marti," Doug said. "Oh, this is Jeremy. Jeremy, this is Sierra."

"Hi," she said. "This is my sister, Tawni."

"Tawni," Jeremy repeated, nodding at her. The double doors to the emergency area swung open, and Katie stepped out. Her right arm was wrapped in gauze and resting in a sling. There appeared to be some sort of salve across her forehead and eyebrows.

"Hey, Doug! Jeremy! What are you guys doing here? Did we make the six o'clock news or something?"

"We were on our way to Tracy's and decided to stop at Bob and Marti's to see if you guys wanted to get together tonight. One of the neighbors was out front and told us what happened. Are you okay?" He rose and carefully gave her a side hug.

"I'm fine. I think the nurse who treated me was in training, and she receives extra credit for every bandage she applies. She wanted to wrap my eyebrows. Can you believe that?"

Doug looked at Katie closely. "What eyebrows?"

"I know," Katie said good-naturedly. "Freaky, huh?"

Sierra noticed that where the light reddish-brown brows had been, Katie now had fine, curly stubble.

"Feel my hair," she offered, lifting a section of the straight, red hair that framed her face. Sierra could see that a large portion had "melted" from the bottom up and stuck out like the wacky, frayed ends of a rope. "And it smells awful."

"Do you know how Todd and Bob are doing?" Sierra asked.

"No. Christy is still in there. I heard one of the doctors talking about sedating Marti. She really flipped out, didn't she?"

"It was pretty gruesome," Sierra said, feeling for some reason she should defend Marti.

"I need to call my parents and ask them some information for the insurance," Katie said. "Do you want to come dial for me, Sierra?"

"Sure."

"I'll come with you," Doug said. "Tracy's probably wondering what happened to us. I'll give her a call, too."

As they walked away, Sierra could hear Jeremy saying to Tawni, "So, do you come here often?"

Tawni laughed.

Jeremy then said, "What an eventful way to start your vacation! Are you staying all week?"

When the three of them returned 20 minutes later from their phone calling, Jeremy and Tawni were still talking.

"Any news?" Doug asked.

Jeremy seemed to have a hard time pulling his

attention away from Tawni to answer Doug. "No, not yet."

"I'm going back in," Katie said. "They'll let me in. And if they don't, I'll whine and say I want my eyebrows bandaged." She made her way through the double doors, being careful not to let her injured arm touch anything along the way.

Sierra slipped in between Jeremy and Tawni and returned to her original seat. It sounded as if the two of them were having a deep, spiritual conversation, something Sierra had rarely heard her sister participate in.

"I think there's room for both," Tawni was saying.

"I do, too," Jeremy agreed. "But don't you find that most Christians today don't think that way?"

"They can always be taught," Tawni said. "I believe the responsibility falls on the people to seek these things out for themselves."

"You're right," Jeremy said.

Sierra wasn't sure what they were talking about, but she was impressed with her sister's approach to the dialogue. She had never seen Tawni talk like this before, especially with a guy.

A few minutes later, Tracy arrived. Sierra introduced her to Tawni as Doug's girlfriend, which extracted an instant smile from both Doug and Tracy but little more than a slight "Hi" from Tawni and Jeremy. They were on the subject of peace in the Middle East now, and it appeared as if the rest of the world barely existed.

"Did they just meet?" Tracy asked quietly. Her sweet,

heart-shaped face reflected the same kind of surprise Sierra was feeling.

Sierra nodded and whispered back, "I've never seen my sister like this."

"I've never seen Jeremy like this either," Tracy said.

# chapter eight

Y NOON THE NEXT DAY, THE CRISIS SEEMED
to have passed. Christy's mom, Margaret,
arrived that morning, which had a calming
effect on Marti. Sierra found it hard to believe that Marti
and Margaret were sisters because they were opposites in
appearance and temperament. Sierra felt an alliance with
Christy's mom. She also must know what it's like to spend
her life in the shadow of a vibrant star for a sister. It made
Sierra wonder if one of them was adopted, the way Tawni
had been adopted in Sierra's family.

The house was full of people when Christy brought
Todd home from the hospital. His right upper arm was
bandaged, and his left arm rested on Christy's shoulder.
He didn't need her support to walk, but neither of
them seemed to mind the roles of "patient" and "nurse."
Christy's mom and Marti followed them into the kitchen,
where Sierra, Tawni, and Katie were sitting around the
counter finishing their late breakfast.

"Give me five," Katie said as Todd entered the kitchen.
She hopped off the stool and held up her free hand, which

Todd swatted with his free hand.

"Does everyone know you're the hero, Katie? You told your mom, didn't you, Christy?" Todd asked.

"That's heroine, if you don't mind, and no," Katie said, her short, silky red hair swishing as she tossed her head. "They all know the truth. You're the hero who saved the day."

"If you hadn't turned off the grill, I think we might have all been blown to Jupiter." Todd sat down and pulled a big, fat dill pickle from the open jar on the counter. He took a bite that snapped the pickle and made Sierra inwardly pucker at the thought of that much dill and vinegar in her mouth.

"How much of your arm got it?" Katie asked.

Todd pointed to an invisible line about three inches down from his shoulder, about the place where his short-sleeved T-shirt ended, and marked again across his elbow. "That much. Not bad. Bob got it much worse. All the way across his left arm, up his neck to his earlobe and the back of his hair."

"It could have been much worse," Christy's mom said. "We're all thankful for the way each of you responded to the emergency."

"I don't know about you guys," Christy said, glancing at Katie and Sierra, "but I felt helpless. I don't know a thing about first aid. If I want to work with little kids, I think I need to know a whole lot more about what to do in a crisis."

"That's right," Katie agreed. "The way preschool kids are today, you never know how many of them might blow up a barbecue during recess."

"You know what I mean," Christy said, giving Katie a playful, exasperated look. "At least you thought to turn off the gas. I never would have thought of that."

"Did the doctor say when Bob might come home?" Marti asked.

"I didn't ask," Todd said. "Are you going over there?"

"Yes," Marti said. "Margaret and I will be there all afternoon. You young people make yourselves at home here, and Tawni, I haven't forgotten about making a call to the agent. I'll phone him on Monday."

"This is much more important," Tawni said. "Don't worry about it, please. You don't have to call him at all."

"No, no, I said I would, and I will. We'll all get through this weekend and then start fresh on Monday. By the way, did the airline ever call about your luggage?"

Sierra held her breath and waited to see how Tawni would respond in front of these strangers. That morning she had acted like a brat, saying she refused to wear the same clothes two days in a row and slamming the bathroom door in Sierra's face when she held out a pair of her shorts and a T-shirt to Tawni. In the end, Sierra's offering was snatched in silence, and Tawni now wore the ragged, cutoff jean shorts and an extra-large, white T-shirt. The outfit was a vast contrast to her usual tailored, belted shorts and tight, scoop-necked T-shirts.

"I was just thinking about calling them again," Tawni said calmly.

"Good idea," Marti said. "I don't suppose any of my clothes would fit you, since you're so much taller than I am, but please feel free to make use of anything you find in my closet. We'll be at the hospital if you need us. Bye, now." Marti made her grand exit with Christy's mom right behind.

Sierra couldn't help but wonder how many times in their lives those two sisters had formed such a train. The image made her even more determined never to fall in line behind Tawni like some kind of shadow.

Christy and Todd began to make sandwiches for themselves while Tawni pulled a slip of paper from her pocket and reached for the phone.

"So, what should we do today?" Katie asked. "Did anyone hear from Doug?"

Tawni put her hand over the mouthpiece and said, "He and Jeremy are at Tracy's. They want us to call them when we decide what we're doing."

"What do you feel up to, Todd?" Christy asked.

"Anything."

"Except surfing, maybe," Katie suggested for him.

"I could wrap my arm in a plastic bag," he said, picking up his sandwich with his left hand. The overly stressed slice of bread on the bottom gave way and dumped half the roast beef and lettuce onto the counter.

"Right," Katie teased. "You can't even get a sandwich in your mouth. How are you going to keep your balance on a surfboard?"

Everyone laughed, and Todd said, "I'll take it one

thing at a time. Sandwich first, then surfboard."

"Until those painkillers wear off," Katie warned. "Then all you'll want to do is take a nap."

"Is that what you guys want to do? Hang out on the beach?" Christy asked.

Sierra had been dying to sink her bare feet into the sand ever since her eyes met the yards and yards of inviting beach stretching to the sea yesterday afternoon. This morning she had almost slipped out for a walk while everyone else was still getting up and dressing, but she'd decided against it in case they wanted to leave for the hospital or something and wouldn't be able to find her. Nothing sounded better to Sierra than spending the afternoon on the beach.

"Sounds great to me," Sierra said.

"Me, too," said Katie. "I want to see what kind of tan I can get where my eyebrows once were."

"I must go shopping," Tawni said, hanging up the phone with a slam. "Still no trace of my luggage. I don't even have a bathing suit!"

"You can borrow one of mine," Sierra said. She was enjoying this much more than she should and realized that if it had been her luggage that was lost, she wouldn't appreciate Tawni offering her clothes every time she opened her mouth. Still, the irony of it was too good to pass up. "I brought several, you know. You can have first pick."

"Oh, let me see. Do I want the one with Tweetie Bird on the front or the gym-class Speedo?" Tawni said.

"You have a Tweetie Bird suit?" Katie said. "Cool."

"No, I don't," Sierra said, deliberately not making eye contact with Tawni so that her icy glare would shatter in midair and all her invisible frozen daggers would fall noiselessly to the ground. "I did when I was 10 or 12. And I've never owned a Speedo."

"My aunt wouldn't mind if you borrowed one of hers. I'm sure she has several to choose from," Christy said.

"You think they would fit?" Tawni asked.

"One way to find out. Come on."

"I'll stay here," Todd said, managing to stuff another bite of his sandwich in his mouth without losing any of it.

"Me, too," Sierra said, placing the lid on the mayonnaise jar and acting as if she had been appointed as the kitchen cleanup crew.

"Not me," said Katie. "An open invitation to go through Marti's closet? Come on, Sierra! Don't you realize this doesn't happen every day?"

"I can live without the experience."

"Suit yourself," Katie said. "Oh, ha! Get it? Suit yourself?" Katie cackled away as the three girls walked out of the kitchen. "Sometimes I crack myself up."

"I guess we should call Doug," Todd said to Sierra. "They might already be on the beach." As he rose to head for the phone, he added, "I'm glad you came. Tawni, too. I'm glad you both came."

Sierra swung open the refrigerator door with more energy than the act required. *Well, I'm not glad she came. I wish I'd never suggested any of this to her. I wish she would find her own friends and leave mine alone. I wish she wasn't so picky and prissy about everything. I wish she wasn't so beautiful and so attractive to guys. I wish* . . . Sierra stopped herself right before she wished something she might regret later.

# chapter nine

*T*HE GREAT THING ABOUT THE BEACH, SIERRA DECIDED, was that it treated everyone the same. Anyone, no matter who she was, could accept the invitation to cradle herself in the warm, rippled sand and feel the sun generously pouring out its gold with the same indifference (or was it benevolence?) on one and all.

Somehow, once she was stretched out on her towel, face toward the heavens, ears drinking in the laughing melody of the ocean's afternoon game of tag, all her envy of Tawni evaporated. These people were still her friends. She was in Southern California, lying on the beach, with a whole week of vacation before her. Sierra refused to sabotage her own holiday.

One other factor calmed her, or at least redirected her focus of energy. When Todd called Doug, he found out that a few more guys had arrived from the San Diego group. That tiny phrase, "a few more guys," rang like a bell inside Sierra. "Anger school is dismissed," it seemed to say. "The class in dreams and wishes is now in session." She remembered what Christy had said on the phone the week before about Sierra possibly meeting someone here this week. One of Doug's friends, maybe. After all, Newport Beach was a wonderful place to meet someone special.

Sierra lay still in the sand, listening to the others talk around her, waiting for Doug and his bunch to show up. What if she opened her eyes and looked for the first time into the face of her future husband? What would he look like? What would his name be? Was she getting carried away with her hopes? Her mom had told her to dream, always dream. It wouldn't hurt to whip up a little dream for herself this afternoon, now would it?

Sierra hadn't allowed herself to do much of this day-dreaming over guys before. Not that she wasn't interested in guys, but she lacked confidence in herself. Growing up in a small community as she had before her family had moved to Portland in January, Sierra had been buddies with every guy in town—not only with the guys who were friends with her older brothers but also with guys her own age. She had known them all since she was in kinder-garten and had thought of them as little more than bullies and buddies.

Since meeting these new friends, and now spending time with them as couples, Sierra's thoughts had certainly turned around. It didn't seem as if she were one of the gang unless she was interested in somebody. So even though she knew that's what motivated her to dream up dating scenarios, she still let herself do it. After all, she was 16. It was time she took her feminine wiles more seriously. Tawni certainly had at that age.

"Jeremy, over here!" Sierra heard her sister call out.

Tawni had done well on her scavenger hunt in Marti's closet, and she now wore a black bathing suit with straps that crisscrossed in the back. It was a bit too small on Tawni and rode up on the sides, but it still looked ravishing on her, of course. She also had borrowed a cover-up trimmed in gold braid that looked like something a movie star would wear while lounging around her Beverly Hills pool. It was, Sierra decided, something she wouldn't be caught dead in.

Sierra could hear the voices of Doug and Tracy as they approached with their group. She hesitated before sitting up and opening her eyes. She had been pumping so much hope into this dream bubble that it seemed almost certain to burst if she even lifted one eyelash and traversed the gulf between dreams and reality.

And burst it did.

Sierra looked up and saw only Doug, Tracy, and Jeremy standing there. No "few more guys" were with them. Tawni went right to work smoothing out a spot for Jeremy's towel next to hers, which was already positioned behind and to the side of everyone else. A private sort of corner for the new couple.

"How's the invalid doing?" Doug teased Todd.

"Rank. The afternoon set is starting to come in," Todd said, casting a longing glance toward the waves. "But Christy won't let me take my board out."

"Oh, right," Christy said. "As if I ever was able to stop you from doing anything."

Sierra thought Christy looked as if she belonged on the beach. She and Todd sat next to each other in matching beach chairs confiscated from Bob and Marti's garage. Christy didn't have a natural "show-off" body like Tawni's, just a round, nicely proportioned shape that looked good in her burgundy bathing suit. The color made her arms and legs look tan, much more tan than Sierra's. On Christy's right wrist was a delicate, gold ID bracelet with the word "Forever" engraved on it. Sierra had heard the story of when Todd first gave her the bracelet and how it had been off and on Christy's wrist over the years. It certainly looked as if it belonged there now.

The other thing Sierra noticed about Christy was that she carried herself well. She didn't "plop" when she sat, the way Katie did. Yet she wasn't petite and graceful like Tracy. She fit somewhere in the middle of those two, which made her approachable and the kind of person who was very watchable. Sierra wished she had a polished, mature look like Christy's rather than her own tomboy appearance.

"What happened to Larry and Antonio?" Todd asked after he seemed to realize that everyone was done giving him sympathy.

"Antonio needed to find a surfboard he could rent for the week," Tracy said, settling down next to Sierra. "Keep an eye out for them. So many people are out today that it'll be hard for them to find us."

"Too bad they wasted their money. They could have used my board," Todd said. Doug had brought a boogie board, which he placed on his towel. Todd's bright-orange surfboard was leaning against the back of his beach chair.

"I'll borrow your surfboard," Katie said, "if you don't mind."

"Sure," Todd said. "I know you'll take good care of Naranja. He's been all over the world with me." He adjusted his position in his chair and flipped on a pair of sunglasses.

Sierra knew *naranja* meant "orange" in Spanish. It made sense that Todd would call it that since it was such a distinctive shade of orange. But she wasn't sure what Todd meant by taking good care of it. It looked pretty beat up to her.

"Katie," Christy said, trying to get her attention, "since when did you start surfing?"

"Ever since I found out Antonio was coming," Katie said with a sparkle in her green eyes. "If he's in the water on a surfboard, then that's where I want to be."

"Who's Antonio?" Sierra asked.

Katie was right next to her, and she turned her head from Christy on her other side to give Sierra the scoop. "Only the most gorgeous college student Italy has ever sent us."

Sierra laughed at Katie's "puppy love" expression.

Christy leaned over and said, "Katie has a thing for exchange students. Did she ever tell you about Michael?"

"He was the one from Ireland, right?"

"Northern Ireland," Katie corrected. "Can I help it if I'm a sucker for a guy with an accent?"

"I take it that it doesn't matter where they're from, as

long as they have an accent," Sierra said.

"Yes," Katie answered, looking over Sierra's head and straining to see two guys walking toward them. "Is that them?"

Everyone looked, including Sierra. She was interested, of course, in how her little dream would turn out. If the "few other guys" consisted of Antonio and Larry, and Antonio was already spoken for, then she wanted to have a good look at Larry.

The two college-aged guys waved and made their way toward the growing group of friends. Sierra guessed Antonio to be the one on the right with the dark hair, and that would mean that Larry was . . .

## *chapter ten*

HUGE! LARRY WAS THE LARGEST GUY SIERRA had ever seen. He had to be a football player. As he approached, she thought he might be Polynesian. His surfboard looked almost like a skateboard under his arm.

Sierra had never thought of herself as a person who identified another individual by his size or skin color. But this guy was very noticeable because of both. In her daydreams, Sierra's potential new boyfriend never looked like Larry.

Everyone was introduced. Sierra smiled and greeted both guys while Katie announced to Antonio that she was going to take Todd's board and hit the waves with them.

"What are we waiting for?" Antonio said. "Let's punch it."

"Don't you mean, 'let's hit it'?" Katie asked, rising and brushing the sand off her backside.

"Larry is always saying 'punch it.' Is that not how you say it?" Antonio's accent would melt any romantic female's heart. He had broad shoulders, straight, white teeth, and engaging eyes. Sierra didn't blame Katie a bit for being attracted to him.

"That's right," Larry agreed in a deep, rumbling voice. "'Punch it.'"

Katie held up her hands in surrender. "Okay by me. Let's punch it."

"You going out, Larry?" Doug asked.

"I sure am. Heather and Gisele are coming up this afternoon. I have a feeling that when Gisele arrives, my week will be scheduled for me. I plan to enjoy my few hours as a free man while I can."

All of Sierra's fragile dreams of a potential romance with either guy fluttered away.

"Women tend to do that to a man's life, don't they?" Doug teased, leaning away from Tracy before she could hit him.

"Hear, hear," Todd said, lifting his bottle of seltzer water in agreement. It seemed to Sierra that Todd looked uncomfortable and a little pale. He wore a long-sleeved T-shirt with the sleeve covering the gauze bandage on his arm. He had tossed a beach towel over his whole right side. The hot sun probably didn't feel too good pounding down its heat on his bandaged burn.

Katie hoisted Todd's surfboard under her arm and trotted down to the water with Antonio right behind her.

"Does she know how to ride that thing?" Larry asked.

"I've given her a few lessons," Todd said. "It's up to you guys to perfect her natural talent." Todd shifted in his chair and slowly stretched, trying to get comfortable.

"Hey, Sierra," Doug said, "you ever ride a boogie board? You can use mine, if you want."

"I think I will," Sierra said, getting up.

Doug, Tracy, and Larry followed her to the water's edge, where the foaming waves came rolling up to their toes, cooling the hot sand. Larry jumped into the water and began paddling out to Kate and Antonio, who were already past where the waves broke. Doug gave a few brief instructions to Sierra on how to hold the board in front of her and lie across it with her feet straight behind her. Then she set out to sea, toward Kate and the guys.

A wave that seemed gigantic to Sierra rose and, like a big hand, closed on top of her, scooting her back to shore. She got up, soaked, still grasping the boogie board, and with a smile to Doug and Tracy, who were watching her, said, "That was my practice run."

"Let me get you past the waves. There are a few tricks to the trade." Doug dove into the oncoming wave and surfaced with his hair slicked back. "Go under," he called back to Sierra.

She followed his advice, and within two waves, she was bobbing with the others in the deeper water. Katie and the guys sat on their boards, floating on the calmer water. Clinging to the boogie board, Sierra realized she couldn't touch the bottom. She was a strong swimmer but hadn't spent much time in the ocean. It felt different from being in the deep part of a lake—maybe because she couldn't see anything in the murky water except clumps of floating kelp that felt slimy when they touched her legs. Sierra wasn't sure she liked this, but she wasn't going to let some globs of seaweed keep her from a new experience.

"I heard there was one down at San Onofre last week that came right up to the surfers," Larry said. "The water's really warm there because of the power plant. It probably attracts them."

"Attracts what?" Doug asked as he treaded water next to Antonio's surfboard. "Jellyfish?"

"No, sharks."

"No way," Sierra squawked.

Everyone looked at her with straight faces. "We get sharks around here every now and then," Doug said. "Not recently—but this *is* their home, you know."

"Why can't they live out there?" Sierra said, bringing her legs closer to the boogie board.

"They have to go where there's food," Doug said. "I saw one here three weeks ago."

"What did you do?" Katie asked.

"I got out of the water, of course."

"Wasn't there one up at Huntington Beach last month?" Larry asked.

"Yeah, did you see it in the paper?" Doug paddled over to Larry's board and held on to the side for support. "There was a bunch of them. Great white, I think. I heard about it from a surfer who said he knew another surfer who was out there. He saw them coming and thought they were dolphins, and then all of a sudden, they attacked him."

"Oh, stop it," Sierra said. "Not really."

Everyone, even Katie, remained serious, silently affirming Doug's story.

"Really," Doug said. "They showed a photo of his board

hacked in half. The guy was in the hospital for a couple of weeks while they tried to reconstruct the lower part of his leg. He said the shark came up from underneath where he was dangling his legs in the water. One big chomp, and his leg was hamburger."

The image forming in Sierra's mind was unpleasant. She tried to brush it away and change the subject. "So, are you going to give me your fine pointers on riding this thing, or do I have to figure it out myself?"

A gentle swell of salty water rose under them and pushed its way to shore.

"That would have been a good wave to catch," Antonio said. Then quickly glancing behind him, he said, "What was that?"

"What was what?" Katie said.

Now Larry snapped his head in the same direction. "I saw it, too. Was that a fish?"

"It was a big fish," Antonio said.

"Where?" Doug tried to boost himself up in the water to see what Larry and Antonio were looking at. "Are you guys putting us on?"

"It's right there!" Antonio said, shooting his arm in the direction of Larry's board. "Don't you see it?"

Sierra wished she were sitting on top of a board herself. She would feel safer and have a better view. She usually wasn't squeamish when it came to animals. Her younger brothers had brought home a variety over the years, including a slimy, yellow banana slug they had put in her bowl of cereal one morning when she left the table for a couple of minutes. She had pretended not to notice and had eaten toast instead of her cereal, which blew all the wind out of Gavin's and Dillon's sails.

This was different. The ocean seemed so huge and deep from where she bobbed in it. And she felt so vulnerable, especially because she couldn't see her own legs in the water.

"You guys are crazy," Doug said. He let go of Larry's board and paddled a few feet away from them, scanning the water. "Just seaweed, you guys. I don't see anything."

He began to swim back toward them when all of a sudden, he let out a blood-chilling scream. His arms went straight up in the air, and then he disappeared, straight down into the water.

"What happened?" Katie yelled.

Sierra was too stunned to speak.

"You guys," Katie hollered, "go get him!"

Antonio dove in with Larry right behind him. Sierra and Katie scanned the water for any sight of the three submerged men. But they didn't see or hear them.

"Where are they?" Katie said frantically.

Sierra stretched her neck and strained her eyes to see anything. Bubbles. Movement. Anything.

Suddenly, she felt something cold and slimy brush against her leg. "Katie!" she screamed.

Before she could form a complete thought, the cold, slimy thing grabbed her right leg and jerked her into the water. The same instant she was going under, she saw Katie topple from her surfboard and fly into the water, shrieking all the way.

# chapter eleven

*A*S SIERRA'S NOSTRILS FILLED WITH WATER, strong hands reached around her waist and boosted her back to the surface. She sucked in a panicked gulp of air and reached for the boogie board floating only a foot away. Doug popped his head out of the water directly in front of her and held on to the other side of the board. A mischievous grin hopscotched across his face.

"Gotcha," he said, laughing wildly. "That was totally awesome!"

Sierra dished out her words slowly between gasping breaths. "That . . . was . . . the . . . worst . . . thing . . . you . . . could . . . have . . . ever . . . done!"

Katie had surfaced right behind Sierra. She wasn't wasting her time with words but went right to work, splashing Larry and Antonio and heaving handfuls of seaweed at them.

"Consider it your initiation to our little circle of friends," Doug said.

"You are a rat!" Sierra said.

"Don't tell Tracy that, will you?" Doug said. "She's

76

crazy about me. I would hate to burst her bubble."

"I think I know now why she stayed on shore."

"You got it. She, Christy, and the others have all gone through their initiation in one form or another, usually involving seaweed, saltwater, and boogie boards. They're our standard operating equipment. Katie, however, keeps falling for it. We've initiated her half a dozen times already."

Sierra noticed Todd's orange surfboard floating out to sea. "Somebody had better grab that board."

The other two guys swam over and climbed back on top of their boards while Doug swam with sure, swift strokes to retrieve Todd's board, which he delivered to a breathless Katie.

"You just wait," Katie panted, glaring at Doug. "One of these days I'm going to get you back so good. You'll see."

"I'm still waiting," Doug teased. "I'm going to be an old, married man before you get around to it."

"Oh?" Sierra said. "Is this an official announcement?"

Doug seemed to turn shy, embarrassed by his own words. "Come on. It's time for you to catch a wave."

Overhead, a small, low-flying airplane came into view. They all looked up as the plane motored overhead, towing a banner that read "Malibu Gold Sunscreen Products."

"What's that?" Sierra asked.

"Advertisement," Katie said. "Haven't you ever seen those before?"

Sierra shook her head.

"It got our attention, didn't it?" Katie said. "Easter vacation, the beach is packed—it's a great way to advertise."

"Check it out," Antonio said. "The swells are really kicking up."

"Don't you mean, 'picking up'?" Katie asked.

"Whatever they're doing, I'm taking the next one," Antonio said, lying on his stomach and paddling toward shore. They watched as he caught the crest of the wave with perfect timing and made a wobbly but successful attempt to stand up. He balanced himself on the board for a full minute and a half before toppling over the side.

"The guy's a natural," Larry said. "Time to show him up. Come on, Katie. Are you with me?"

"As long as you don't have any more shark attacks up your sleeve."

They paddled together quickly to catch the next wave. Larry caught the edge of it but couldn't get up. Katie missed it, too. Then, as Sierra watched, Katie quickly repositioned herself for the next wave, which she caught and rode to shore on her knees. Maybe she didn't want to push her luck by attempting to stand, so she had stayed low.

Tracy, who was standing ankle deep in the foaming water, applauded Katie as she came to shore. Sierra liked being part of this group, practical jokes and all. She loved trying new things and determined that once she had mastered the boogie board, she was going to trade it in for a ride on that magical orange surfboard.

The boogie board turned out to be a breeze for her. Doug only had to run through the basics with her once, and she caught wave after wave, with Doug bodysurfing beside her, looking like a maniac otter. She loved the sensation, loved the pull and push of the mighty ocean giving her free rides. Sierra thought it would be great to live by the ocean and play like this all the time.

Quite a while later, she decided it was time to take a break. Doug said he'd had enough for a while, too, so they headed toward shore. They passed Katie paddling out with Antonio as they took their last ride in.

"What are the chances of that relationship working out?" Sierra asked Doug as they wrung the water from their hair at the shoreline and walked back to the group on the sand.

"I stopped trying to figure relationships out a long time ago. Tracy says I'm clueless. She's probably right. The only couple I'd put any guarantees on would be Todd and Christy."

"And you and Tracy," Sierra added, spotting Tracy a few yards ahead, waving at them from her beach chair.

"Yeah, me and Tracy." His voice turned deep.

Sierra glanced over to see a tender look spread across his face. He looked more mature at that moment than she had ever seen him, even with the drops of water clinging to his eyelashes and the goofy way his soaked hair stuck out on the left side. Sierra took note. *This is the look of a man in love.*

"She's the most awesome person in the world," he said, watching Tracy stand up and come toward him with a dry towel in her hand.

Sierra made another note. *And there's a woman in love. I can't believe it. I'm surrounded!*

"Hey," she said, breaking up the sweet moment between Doug and Tracy, "what happened to everyone else?"

"Todd was starting to feel the pain in his arm, although he wouldn't admit it. Christy coaxed him into going back to the house with her. She said she wanted to call the hospital and check on Bob. I'm sure she was also going to convince Todd to take it easy, like the doctor told him to."

"What about my sister?"

"She persuaded Jeremy to take her shopping," Tracy said.

Doug wrapped the towel around his shoulders and reached into their small cooler for something to drink. "Jeremy went shopping?"

"I know," Tracy said. "Would you like something to drink, Sierra?"

"Sure. Anything."

Doug handed her a can of Squirt and said, "Man, Jeremy must have it bad! He went to the Ice Capades once when he had a crush on a girl last year, but shopping? This is pretty serious."

"And what's wrong with the Ice Capades?" Sierra challenged, stretching out on her stomach and letting her back "solar" dry.

"It's a chick thing," Doug said.

"Please," Tracy interjected, "don't get him started."

Before Doug could make another comment, an airplane engine roared over them, and Tracy asked, "What does that say?"

Sierra rolled over and sat up. Shielding her eyes from

the lowering sun, she read the banner strung behind the advertising plane. "Good Earth-something," she said.

"Good Earth Restaurants," Doug said. "Sounds good to me. I'm starved."

"Do you want to go back to the house?" Tracy asked Doug. "Christy might appreciate it if you could help her convince Todd he needs to take his medicine and rest."

"Sure. I'm ready. Are you, Sierra?"

Sierra decided to wait for Katie and the guys. Doug and Tracy left their ice chest full of drinks for the others and walked away, hand in hand.

*Let's see . . .* Sierra began reviewing for herself. *Doug and Tracy are in love, Todd and Christy are in love, Tawni and Jeremy are something. They're together, at any rate. Katie is interested in Antonio, and Larry said his girlfriend is coming up tonight. Am I the leftover pork chop here or what?*

She lay with her face to the sun, trying to decide if she should feel sorry for herself. She logically reminded herself that she was younger than anyone else in the gang. She also consoled herself with the reminder that Randy was taking her out next Friday. At least she was being asked out. It wasn't as if she had no attention from guys.

It was Tawni, really, who prompted all the jealous feelings. Todd and Christy belonged together. She had watched Doug and Tracy get together in England. And she couldn't wish for a better guy for Katie than Antonio. But why did Tawni deserve an instant boyfriend? What if Tawni hadn't come? Would Jeremy have been interested in Sierra instead? He was great-looking, intelligent, and slightly serious, and he seemed to be a strong Christian. Would she have been attracted to him? Would Jeremy have thought that Sierra was too young to take seriously, the way Paul had brushed her off on the way home from England once he had found out how young she was?

Sierra loved the way the sun dried and warmed her all over. Even though she was lying still, it felt as if she were riding another wave. The sensation was similar to the way she felt after getting off a roller coaster. It was a sensation she liked, and it made her smile.

The late afternoon breeze began to pick up, bringing a sudden chill with it. Slipping into her beach cover-up, one of Dad's old, white, long-sleeved shirts, Sierra rolled up the sleeves and turned up the collar on her sunburnt neck.

Katie and the guys were making their way through the sand with the boards under their arms. Katie's face was shining as she carefully laid Todd's board on her towel. "Did you see that last one?"

"No, sorry. I missed it."

"I finally stood up all the way! This is a breakthrough for me, Sierra. And you missed it!"

"We saw it," Antonio said teasingly. "It wasn't anything to call home about."

"Antonio, we say 'write home about,'" Katie corrected him.

"You can write if you want," he said. "I think calling is faster."

Sierra let out a giggle. Katie was the only one who didn't see that Antonio liked getting a reaction out of her. Sierra imagined his mind was working overtime trying to find ways to mix up expressions just to keep Katie attentive.

"Gisele wants to go to the Old Spaghetti Factory for dinner tonight. You guys want to join us?" Larry was looking at Antonio and Katie.

Katie cast an almost shy glance at Antonio. At least it looked as shy as Sierra had ever seen Katie appear to be.

"Sure, we would love to," he answered for both of them.

Katie smiled at Antonio. Antonio smiled back. Larry flipped the lid on the ice chest and asked, "Are these up for grabs?"

"Yes." Sierra swallowed the strong feelings that rose from her stomach to her throat. They hadn't asked her to go with them, had they? It sounded to her like a double date. If she went, she would be the oddball—again.

For the first time, she missed Amy, Randy, and her other friends in Portland. She thought of the wacky Saturday morning at the water fountain, and she realized she felt like Peanut, trying to keep up with Brutus. Maybe someone should stick her in a backpack and pull her out when the week was over.

"I'm going to head back to the house," Sierra said.

"Okay. We'll see you later," Larry said. "Nice meeting you, Sarah."

Sierra was about to correct him but then decided it wasn't worth it.

# chapter twelve

OB AND MARTI'S HOUSE WAS FULL OF ACTIVITY when Sierra entered through the sliding glass door off the patio. Tawni, Jeremy, and Aunt Marti were in the living room, and Tawni was pulling new clothes from a shopping bag.

"Sierra," Tawni said, her face full of excitement, "you won't believe the selection of stores they have here! I found everything in record time."

"I bet you were glad for that," Sierra said to Jeremy, giving him a sympathetic look.

"We had a great time," Jeremy said.

For one instant, Sierra wondered if this guy was actually a well-constructed robot. Did she detect a hint of a metallic resonance in his "We had a great time"? He looked human enough. As a matter of fact . . . Sierra looked at him more closely. Something was strangely familiar about Jeremy. She couldn't place it, but across his eyes and around his mouth, he looked like someone she knew.

"How's Bob doing?" Sierra asked, forcing herself to look away from Jeremy and at Marti.

"Better, I think. They're still trying to make a decision about the skin graft. I wish they would decide. He's been sleeping all day, poor thing."

Marti seemed like a different woman from the one who had fainted only 24 hours ago—more calm and relaxed. Sierra still wasn't sure she liked her.

"What's everyone else doing?"

"I made Todd go home to rest," Marti said, her hand drawing up to her hip. "He's acting as if nothing happened to him when in reality he should still be in the hospital. At least he would take his medication and get some sleep."

"Did Doug and Tracy go home, too?"

"I think so. Christy's in the kitchen. She can give you a full report. I returned only a few minutes ago myself." Then, turning to Tawni, she said, "As I was saying, I wish you would have let me know you were going shopping. I have a personal shopper, you see. I could have given her a call, and she could have done all the legwork for you."

Sierra slid out of the living room and went to the kitchen, where she found Christy and her mom sitting at the round kitchen table. They seemed to be in a close conversation, so Sierra waved her hand and said, "I'm going upstairs to take a shower."

"Okay," Christy said. "I'll be up in a bit."

Sierra headed upstairs and pulled some clean clothes from her corner of the crowded guest room. The shower felt good, and it amazed her to see so much sand swirling around the drain. Even after she was out of the shower and dressed, she found more sand in her left ear.

It was quiet in the guest room. She stood by the window and looked out at the beach. The crowds from that afternoon had thinned. In the endless sky, the clouds topped the ever-churning, gray-green ocean like gigantic dollops of whipping cream. "It's beautiful," Sierra whispered.

Just then the bedroom door opened, and in tumbled Katie and Tawni, laughing like old chums.

"Guess what?" Katie said to Sierra. "Tawni says she's going to glamorize me for our big date tonight. She thinks she can draw in new eyebrows!"

"I'm sure she can," Sierra said.

"What's that supposed to mean?" Tawni snapped.

"It means, if anyone can draw in new eyebrows for Katie, I'm sure you're the best person for the job," Sierra said, sounding innocent as she defended herself. Why was it that Tawni could read even the slightest pinch of sarcasm in Sierra's comments?

Tawni looked as if she were about to say something and then changed her mind. "I'll be only a minute in the shower," Tawni said to Katie.

Sierra wanted to say, "Since when?" but she held her tongue.

"I'll take my shower downstairs," Katie suggested, reaching into her disheveled bag for some clothes. "What are you going to wear tonight, Sierra?"

"This." She looked down at her baggy jeans and striped T-shirt.

"I don't know what to wear. Did you see Tawni's new outfit?"

Sierra forced out a "Yes, it's great" just as Tawni slipped into the bathroom and closed the door.

"The Old Spaghetti Factory isn't a very fancy place. Have you ever been there?"

"No." Sierra's discomfort with the arrangements for the evening grew. She wasn't sure she was actually invited to this dinner. The last thing she wanted to do was be the only one there without a date.

Fortunately, Christy walked in and said, "Are you talking about the Spaghetti Factory?"

"Yes. You and Todd are going, aren't you?" Katie asked. "What are you going to wear?"

"We're not going. Todd needs to take it easy, and I thought I'd keep my mom and aunt company tonight. We'll probably go back to the hospital. You guys go ahead. It's a fun place." Christy came over to Katie's bag and pulled out a shirt. "Wear this," she suggested. "I always liked this one on you."

"'Liked' is the key word here," Katie said. "Do you realize how long I've had this relic? I need to go shopping."

"That's a new one," Christy said. "You hate shopping."

"I hate looking like a slob more."

Sierra couldn't help but wonder what other bits of advice her sister had used on Katie to plant the word "slob" in her brain. It was definitely a "Tawni" word, and one she often used on Sierra.

"You can borrow anything of mine you want," Christy suggested.

"What I'd really like to wear is one of Sierra's skirts," Katie said.

The admission surprised and flattered Sierra.

"You're welcome to whatever you can find in there," Sierra said.

"Did you bring that one you wore in Belfast? The one with the silver threads woven through it?"

"It's in there," Sierra said. "Help yourself. There's a matching vest with silver trim, if you want to borrow that, too."

"Cool, cool, cool," Katie said, pawing through Sierra's clothes. "You have the coolest clothes of anyone I've ever met. And I love your jewelry."

"Borrow whatever you like."

"Thanks, Sierra. What a pal!"

Sierra wouldn't admit it, but inwardly she couldn't wait to see Tawni's expression when Katie showed up, ready for her makeup, wearing one of Sierra's outfits.

"Are you going with them?" Christy asked.

"No. I . . ." She didn't know how to say it without sounding like she felt sorry for herself. "I'd rather stick around here tonight."

"You won't mind being here alone if we go to the hospital, will you?"

"Whatever works out is fine with me." Those were polite words, not words from her heart. What Sierra wanted was to be invited to be part of somebody's group, even if it was the group of women going to the hospital.

"You're welcome to come with us," Christy said, as if reading Sierra's thoughts. "I can't promise that it'll be very exciting."

"I don't need exciting," Sierra said. "Just an invitation, and I'll take yours."

Christy studied Sierra's face. "Are you okay?"

"Sure! Fine. Great, actually! It's really beautiful here. I loved being on the beach today. And the water was fantastic. I had a really good time." Even though Sierra felt certain she could trust Christy with her true feelings, she didn't want to pour out all her insecurities and put any more stress on Christy than she already felt.

"It looks like you got a little sunburnt," Christy said, touching her finger to her own nose. "I wasn't out long enough to get pink. You should have seen me the first time I came here, though. It was in the summer, and I fried my first day out. Like a lobster! It doesn't feel that hot when you're lying out because of the breeze."

"I know," Sierra agreed. Before she could say anything else, someone rapped long fingernails on the closed door.

"Come in," Christy called. But the door opened before the words were out of her mouth.

Marti gave the room a quick surveillance and seemed surprised. By Sierra's standards of cleanliness, there was nothing wrong with the room. But Christy must have sensed something different, because she immediately said, "We'll clean it up."

"Oh, I'm not worried," Marti said, dramatically stepping over the wet bath towel Sierra had left wadded up by her futon bed on the floor. She realized how rude that must appear to Marti. "The maid is coming the day you all leave, so I'm not worried about a thing." She added, "I wanted to ask you, Christy darling, if you had a preference of where to go for dinner tonight."

"It doesn't matter to me," Christy said. "Sierra is staying home with us. Do you have a preference, Sierra?"

"What about that restaurant advertised on the airplane banner—the Good Earth?"

"Wonderful choice," Marti said, casting her fickle approval on Sierra for the first time. "Let's plan to leave here in, say, 15 minutes."

"We'll be ready," Christy said.

"How about you, Sierra dear? Will you have enough time to change, or should we plan on 20 minutes instead of 15?"

"I'm ready to go now," Sierra said, not liking this woman one bit.

"Really?" Marti raised a finely shaped eyebrow.

Sierra didn't know how to answer without sounding rude. She was used to Tawni's occasional comments on her taste in fashion, but for this woman Sierra barely knew to show her obvious distaste was incredible. A half dozen stinger phrases raced through Sierra's mind. Her mother had told her once that it wasn't a sin when those thoughts came to her, but what she did with them determined whether or not they would be classified as sinning. Sierra decided not to take any chances, and she let each of the rude comments fly out the back side of her brain as quickly as they had flown in.

As the bad thoughts were on their way out, another one flew in. It was Todd's comment on the patio when he had said that Marti needed Jesus.

"I'll be glad to change," Sierra said, amazed to hear such words come from her own mouth. "Do you have any suggestions of what would be appropriate?"

Marti appeared so caught off guard that she only smiled and said, "Wear whatever you like, dear." With her dignity still intact, Marti turned. As she exited the room, she called over her shoulder, "Downstairs then, in 15 minutes."

Christy looked surprised. "I wish I'd learned to do that years ago. I admire you, Sierra."

"You wouldn't if you knew what I was really thinking."

## chapter thirteen

SIERRA LEARNED SOME HARD LESSONS THAT NIGHT and the next day. She learned that it's best to sit and listen when you're the guest, especially when Marti is the one treating you to dinner. It's also helpful to pretend to be asleep when your sister and friend come in from their night out. They will divulge plenty of information while brushing their teeth, which is easier to hear when they're not looking at your face, reading your expression, especially since they both had a wonderful time. All Sierra could do was wish she had been with them, with some terrific guy paying lots of attention to her.

Marti had made an appointment for Tawni with the modeling agent on Monday. When they returned late that afternoon, Sierra, Christy, and Todd had just come up from the beach and were sitting on the patio with Christy's mom. Christy reminded Todd for the second time that he needed to take his next pill.

Sierra had settled comfortably into a patio chair next to Todd when Marti and Tawni stepped onto the patio. Sierra felt sure she would soon have her own pill to swallow: the news that Tawni's career into fame and fortune was about to be launched.

"Before anyone says anything," Tawni said, "I'm not going to pursue this. There's too much required for a job in modeling. I'd have to move and completely commit myself to making it. I'm not interested in doing that."

"Really?" Sierra wasn't sure if she sounded as shocked as she felt. She never doubted that Tawni had what it took to be a great model and that she would probably be successful at it. But Tawni had never been much of a risk taker. Unless she was 100 percent sure of something, she rarely took a chance. She must have had serious doubts about succeeding at this, and her insecurities had taken over, drowning out the possibilities.

"He said she was a natural," Marti said, not trying to hide her disappointment. "I knew she was. Maybe you people can talk some sense into her."

None of them said a word. Marti threw up her hands and said, "I tried. No one can say I didn't try."

"And I told you I appreciated it," Tawni said. "It's just not for me."

Marti didn't respond.

"Bob called while you were out," Christy's mom said. "I told him we would go over to the hospital as soon as you came back. Whenever you're ready to go, I'm ready."

"I'm ready now," Marti said. "I probably should have been there all afternoon." The two women left, giving instructions that the group was on its own for dinner that night.

"Did Jeremy call?" Tawni asked.

"He said he would stop by after five," Todd said. "A bunch of us are going roller-blading, in case you two want to come."

"Sounds fun. But you're not going, are you, Todd? Not with your arm still bandaged like that."

"I probably shouldn't," Todd said with a look of frustration. "Christy will get all over my case."

"Why do you say that?" Christy challenged him. She didn't look like she was teasing. "You talk as if I'm treating you like a baby."

Sierra saw a fight brewing. Tawni excused herself and went inside. Sierra wanted to, but the leg of her patio chair was wedged with Todd's, and she couldn't scoot her chair back from the table unless he moved his first. At the moment, he was busy.

"Aren't you?" Todd replied.

"No, I'm not treating you like a baby," Christy said. "I'm trying my best to do whatever I can to help you."

"I know," he said.

If he had left it there, Sierra imagined the argument would have been diffused, and they could have gone back to their casual, friendly conversation. But Todd had to add, "Just like your aunt."

Christy's face turned deep red. "What is that supposed to mean?"

Todd's jaw seemed to stick out defiantly as he retorted, "I can take care of myself." Then, toning down his voice, he glanced at Sierra and pushed back his chair, saying,

"Excuse me. I need to take my medicine." He strode into the house, slamming closed the patio's sliding door.

Sierra felt uncomfortable. She knew Christy must feel awkward, too. "You okay?" Sierra ventured.

Christy looked as if she were about to cry. "Can you believe it? We've never had a fight like this before. I've never seen him act this way." Tears glistened in the corners of her eyes.

"He's in a lot of pain with the burn, I'm sure," Sierra said. "The medication can do weird things to him, too. It did for my grandma after her surgery. She said a lot of strange things and snapped at my mom all the time the first week she was home from the hospital. I'm sure Todd didn't mean anything by it."

"No, he did. And he's probably right. I have been acting like my aunt, trying to take care of him. It's just that there's no one else to do it. His dad works all the time, and his mom is remarried and lives in Florida. He's been on his own for years."

"Well," Sierra ventured, "then maybe it's hard for him to get used to having someone else do stuff for him. He's probably not used to having you around all the time."

"But I'm not around. We only see each other on weekends. I thought we were so close," Christy said, wiping a tear from her cheek. "I guess our relationship isn't as far along as I thought. Don't fall in love, Sierra. It complicates even the best friendships."

"I may be way off here," Sierra said, "but if you two only see each other on weekends, then this is probably really good for you. I mean, it's Monday, so you've seen each other for longer than usual, and the circumstances have been pretty stressful."

Christy nodded.

"I'm just saying that this is giving you both a chance to strengthen your relationship by working through this problem. That's not a bad thing, is it? I mean, all couples have arguments. Why don't you go talk to him? I'm sure you can work this out."

"I think you're right, Sierra," Christy said. "We've talked about this before. Ever since we came back from Europe, we've had this fairy-tale feeling about our relationship. We've been saying that we want God to test it and see if it's real and strong and lasting."

Sierra smiled and reached over to give Christy's arm a squeeze. "Didn't anyone ever tell you not to pray for stuff like that? The answer is always trials. Sounds like that's what's happening with you guys. You pray for God to strengthen your relationship, and look at what you get."

"You're right," Christy agreed. After a comfortable pause, she said, "I'm glad you're here. Thanks for coming down. You know, I really appreciate your encouragement. How did you become so wise?"

"Well, it wasn't from personal dating experience, that's for sure," Sierra joked.

"Your chance will come." Christy rose gracefully. "Don't you wish it on yourself too soon though, okay?"

"As if I had a choice," Sierra muttered as Christy left her alone on the patio. Fortunately, Katie showed up a few minutes later to ask Sierra if she wanted to go roller-blading with them that evening.

Sierra agreed to go. Todd and Christy stayed behind, saying they were going to have dinner with his dad. From the expressions on their faces, it didn't appear that they had worked out their differences yet.

The gang rented roller blades at a little shop by the pier and buddied up as they raced along the miles of sidewalk separating the rows of beachfront houses from the sand. Sierra tried to be cheerful as she saw Jeremy reach for Tawni's hand and the two take off laughing. She watched Doug tie Tracy's skates for her and smiled to see how much shorter Gisele was than Larry. Katie persisted in telling Antonio they were skating on the "sidewalk" not the "boardwalk."

Sierra tried to find a buddy for herself. She felt as if she were back in grade school, and the time had come to pick teams, but she was one of the last to be picked. Only, this had never happened to her. She was always the team leader and did the picking. For a few minutes, she considered writing notes of apology to those less athletic kids whom she had picked last all those years.

"Are you ready to go?" a friendly voice asked her. It was Heather, a thin, shy member of the gang whose wispy, blond hair was whipping across her face in the evening breeze. Heather pulled a few strands out of her mouth and said, "Your name is Sierra, right?"

"Right. And you're Heather?"

She nodded. "I bet you're a pro at this. It's not my

favorite activity, so if I make a complete fool of myself, you can go on without me. I'll understand."

"I'm sure you'll do fine," Sierra said. "Keep telling yourself to glide. Don't try to pick up your feet. There you go. Exactly. Come on, we can catch up with those Ricky Racers."

For the next two hours, Sierra had a blast laughing with Heather, playing tag with the other couples, and showing off her coordination skills by skating backward. She nearly collided with a man and his terrier but was able to inch past them by leaning way back. The wind felt cool against her sunburnt cheeks. She didn't mind a bit that it was also whipping her hair into knots.

As the sun set, Sierra decided this had been a memorable day. In the morning, she had given surfing a try and had managed to stand all the way up for three seconds before crashing into the water. She would have tried some more, but her arms ached at the shoulders, and anyway, there was always tomorrow.

The gang returned the skates, and all decided to go over to Balboa Island for hot dogs at some place Doug liked. Sierra piled into the backseat of Larry's car along with Katie and Antonio. The hot dog place turned out to be a tiny stand that sold only hot dogs, frozen bananas, and "world-famous" Balboa Bars—creamy vanilla ice cream bars dipped in chocolate. Tracy teased Doug about being a real gourmet. Then everyone else teased him when he ordered six jumbo hot dogs and had no problem wolfing them down. He even went back for dessert.

Sierra managed to eat one of the jumbo dogs, but it didn't settle well, so she decided against dessert. When everyone was finished, they walked en masse down the shop-lined street, peering in the windows and laughing all the way.

Sierra hung out with Katie and Antonio, smiling when she saw Antonio slip his arm around Katie's shoulder. But his action also made her suddenly feel out of place all over again. They still included her in their conversation and acted as if they enjoyed having her with them. Still, they were becoming a couple, just like her sister and Jeremy, who were strolling with their arms around each other.

The next day, Todd and Christy joined the group on the beach late in the afternoon, but Sierra couldn't tell if they had settled things between them. The baseball cap she was wearing to shade her already peeling nose from the sun also shaded her view of the couple. She hoped they were getting along okay.

Just then, Doug and Antonio came up from the water with their boards under their arms. As Doug dropped his boogie board next to Tracy's towel, it knocked sand all over her. Immediately, she sprang up, wiping her eyes.

"Are you okay?" Sierra asked.

"I think I have some sand in my eye," Tracy said. "Can you see it?"

"Look," Doug said. "Here it comes." The sound of an airplane whirred in the distance.

Sierra leaned closer to Tracy, flipping up the brim of her cap so she wouldn't bump Tracy's forehead. "Try opening your eye," she said.

Tracy's eyelid fluttered, and she said, "I can feel it. In my right eye."

"Trace," Doug called. "Look up. You have to see this."

"Just a second. I have something in my eye."

"Look to the left," Sierra said.

"Do you need some eyedrops?" Heather asked. "I have some."

"I see it," Sierra said. "Right along the lower lid. Don't blink."

The airplane engine roared closer. "Come on, Trace," Doug said. "You can't miss this!"

Now Todd was shouting at her, too. "Tracy, look at the plane!"

"Just a minute!" she yelled, taking the eyedrops from Heather. Two other girls huddled around her, asking if they could help.

"You're going to miss it!" Doug yelled. He stepped over, took her by the arm and pulled her up to his side. "Look!"

Tracy blinked, and in an irritated voice said, "What are you doing, Doug? I have something in my eye!"

"Just look at the plane for one second!" Todd yelled.

"Tracy, read the banner!" Larry called.

Sierra turned to see what the men were so worked up about. The plane was nearly past them, but the words on the banner were clear. It read, "Tracy, will you marry me?"

## chapter fourteen

INSTANTLY, THE WHOLE GROUP WAS CROWDING around Doug and Tracy. Tracy was crying, and Doug had his wet arm around her shoulders. He offered her his T-shirt to wipe her eyes, but she opted for the corner of the big T-shirt she was wearing over her bathing suit.

"Now you know what I was talking to your dad about last weekend," Doug said. "He's all for it. Of course your mom is, too. So are my parents."

"Tracy, I'm so happy for you!" Heather said, wiggling into the huddle and hugging her.

"Just a minute, Heather," Doug said. "She hasn't told me yes yet."

Everyone grew quiet, moving back slightly to give the couple some room. Tracy looked at Doug with tears still streaming down her cheeks. "Well," she joked nervously, "at least it got the sand out of my eye."

Doug looked at her patiently, waiting for her answer.

Sierra wondered if the crowds of people on the beach staring at them because of all the commotion had any idea what was going on. The onlookers didn't bother Doug a bit. He stood like a rock, unwilling to move until Tracy gave him the answer he and everyone else in the group wanted to hear.

Tracy's expression grew soft. She looked into Doug's eyes, and tilting her heart-shaped face toward his, she whispered, "Yes, yes, a thousand times yes . . . you big lug!" Then with a playful thump on his chest, she said, "What if I hadn't looked at the plane?"

"I guess I would have had to pay the guy to come back tomorrow," Doug said. "Either that or find some other Tracy on the beach who *was* paying attention." He wrapped his arms around her, and they hugged.

"Isn't he going to kiss her?" Tawni said quietly to Sierra.

Jeremy was the one who answered. "No, not until their wedding day."

"You mean they've never kissed?"

"Doug's never kissed any girl," Sierra said.

"You're kidding!" Tawni said. "Isn't that taking purity a bit far?"

"Tracy doesn't think so," Sierra said quickly. "And neither do I."

"That's because you've never been kissed," Tawni said. "You wouldn't know."

Sierra blushed and felt like sinking into the sand. How could Tawni say that in front of Sierra's friends? Fury began to boil inside. It was one thing to decide you weren't going to kiss anyone, like Doug had, and a completely different thing to have your sister announce that no one had even tried to kiss you.

Sierra felt as if she didn't belong with this group. Here they all were, going to college and becoming engaged, while she stuck out like a two-year-old. She wished she were home, planning her first big date with Randy and taking her time to grow up.

"Over here, honey," a male voice called out behind them. The man was wearing a blue baseball cap and holding a video camera. A blond-haired woman beside him came rushing up to give Tracy a hug. Apparently, they were her parents, and they were in on the scheme.

"Did you see the plane, Mom?" Tracy asked.

"Of course. Your father captured the whole thing on tape. We were about ready to start yelling for you to look up, too!"

Another set of parents, quite obviously Doug's by the strong father-son resemblance, made their way through the sand and told the whole group to smile while Doug's mom snapped photos. Lots of hugs and picture taking took place before Tracy and Doug left with their parents for what Tracy's mom called their "celebration dinner."

"I wonder when they'll get married," Katie said after the commotion had passed and everyone had settled back on the towels and beach chairs.

"Soon, if Doug gets his wish," Todd said with a smile. "He graduates in a few months."

"So do you," Katie challenged. With a twinkle in her eye, she looked at Christy and then back at Todd. "Any chance of a double wedding?"

Todd looked fondly at Christy. "I don't think so."

Sierra noticed that Christy didn't seem upset by his words, although Sierra couldn't help but wonder how their argument from the day before had ended up.

Todd reached over and covered Christy's hand with his. "I have some growing up to do," he admitted to the group. "Christy and I had a long talk about it yesterday. Do you mind my telling them?" Todd asked her.

Christy shook her head. Sierra thought Christy's cheeks were turning red.

"You might as well," Katie said. "Otherwise we'll have to drag it out of Christy later tonight in our room under threat of a pillow war. She's not exceptionally cooperative about these things, so it might be in her best interest if you tell us now."

"I've pretty much been on my own since my parents divorced. This accident has been a good thing in that it has shown me I need to learn how to accept love from another person."

"That person being, perhaps, Christy?" Katie interjected in her spunky way.

Todd gave Christy another tender smile. "Of course Christy. There isn't anyone else. There never has been."

Sierra thought her heart was going to melt all over the sand, and she would have to scoop it up in her towel, take it to the house, and put it in the refrigerator before she could get it back inside her. She couldn't imagine a guy ever looking at her like that or saying those kinds of things to her.

"So, when I finish school, it looks as if I'm going to

move down to Escondido, or at least near there, so Christy and I can get to know each other on a more consistent basis. Our relationship has always been in little pieces of time, separated by long stretches of being apart. We need to see how we do in average, day-to-day life."

"Isn't that what you find out once you're married?" Larry said. "What's wrong, Todd? Are you afraid to take any chances?"

Sierra realized she wasn't the only one who assumed Todd and Christy would end up getting married. Everyone else seemed to think the same thing.

"You probably wouldn't ask that if your parents were divorced," Todd said. "It's like I said, I have a few things to learn about loving another person for the rest of my life and letting that person love me. I've been too much of a loner for too long."

No one said anything at first. They all knew he meant what he said. It made Sierra imagine how deep Todd's love for Christy must be. He wasn't willing to make any mistakes, even if it meant waiting to get married.

"I give him six months max before he proposes," Larry said.

Christy glanced shyly at Todd.

"You're on," Katie said, reaching over and slapping Larry a high five.

"Get me five," Antonio said, holding up his hand to Katie.

"You mean, 'give me five,'" Katie corrected him. "Not 'get me.'"

"Oh, are you saying you're getting sodas from that ice chest over there?" Antonio teased. "Then I don't need five; I only need one. But perhaps my friends are thirsty as well. Larry? Gisele? What would you like? Katie's getting five."

# chapter fifteen

S IERRA HAD A LOT OF THINKING TIME THE NEXT
morning. Today and tomorrow were her last days
at the beach, and so many things still seemed to be
tied up in knots inside of her. She hadn't settled a thing
with Tawni. Her jealousy seemed only to grow when
Tawni and Jeremy had gone out alone last night for a long
walk on the beach.

Her feelings of being a misfit kept her from sleeping
well; so she was up at 6:00. She quietly slipped into her
clothes and went downstairs. After pouring herself a glass
of orange juice, she settled into the plush, white sofa in the
living room, watching through the huge picture windows
as the day began to wake up.

She prayed. She thought. She sipped her orange juice
and prayed some more. Quiet footsteps padded down the
stairs. Sierra watched the doorway and was surprised to
see Christy.

"Hi," Christy whispered.

"Hi."

"Am I disturbing you?"

"No, not at all. I was just praying through some stuff."

"Do you mind if I ask you a question?" Christy said, sitting down beside Sierra. "Is Tawni one of the things you're praying about?"

"Yes. How did you know?"

"I don't have a sister, so I've never had to go through the kinds of things you and Tawni go through, but I think I know how you must feel sometimes."

"I'm jealous," Sierra said bluntly. "I know what the problem is, and I know it's wrong, but I don't know how to fix it. I try so hard to change my feelings and thoughts, but they keep coming back, even stronger."

"I know what that's like," Christy said.

"Somehow I find it hard to believe you've ever been jealous of anyone," Sierra said.

"You'd be surprised if you knew. As a matter of fact, I'm going to tell you. It was Tracy."

"Tracy?"

"I find it hard to believe now, too," Christy said. "When I first met Tracy, she and Todd were really close friends. I was so jealous of her. She and Todd gave me a Bible for my birthday, and I almost threw it back in her face. She even made me a fabric cover for it. Can you believe that?"

"No. When I met you two in England, you seemed like best friends who had never had a fight."

"Relationships take time, Sierra. That's what Todd and I are finding out. I think the main thing I'm learning is that it doesn't help to try harder. Remember what Todd said the other day about my being like Marti because I was trying so hard? The only thing that works is surrendering—giving up all your rights and expectations and asking God to do a God-thing in your relationship."

"Is that what happened with you and Tracy?"

"I guess so. Sort of. What helped me the most was when I got to know her. I realized she and Todd were just good friends, and when I started to understand her, it was a lot easier to become her friend."

"You know what's really pathetic?" Sierra said. "I hardly know my sister. I mean, we live in the same house, but I don't understand her at all. Maybe I do need to pray about this differently. Instead of asking God to change her, maybe I should try surrendering our relationship to Him and ask Him to do . . . what did you call it?"

"A God-thing. It's Katie's word. It means when something happens that you can't explain and you know that God was the One doing it."

"You mean like you and Todd ending up together in Spain."

A smile dawned over Christy's face. "Exactly."

Sierra couldn't help but notice that Christy was a natural beauty. Here it was, early morning, and her eyes sparkled and her skin glowed. Though uncombed, her hair hung soft and natural from the crown of her head.

"Thanks," Sierra said. "I appreciate your advice."

"You know what's funny? Todd used to have this kind of spiritual discussion with me, and I'd never quite understand what he was saying. You're a lot more spiritually sensitive than I was at your age."

Christy's words acted as a bleak reminder that a gap of nearly three years existed between them. It brought up all those sinking feelings of not fitting in. Sierra's expression must have changed because Christy reached over and patted her arm, saying, "I meant that as a compliment."

Sierra gave her a forced smile and said, "I know. Thanks. It's just that I've felt pretty high-schoolish being around all you guys this week. It didn't feel that way in England, but now I realize how much I'm behind the rest of you in experience and age."

"I don't think of it that way."

"I don't know, Christy. Have you ever felt as if you were caught between two lives? The one you're living, and the one you wish you were living?"

"I think everyone feels like that at one time or another. I know I did a couple of summers ago when I was a counselor at summer camp. I left home that week dreaming of adventure, romance, and great spiritual victories. I came home wanting all the familiar people and places in my life and wishing the old things would never change."

"Do you think we're ever happy?" Sierra said, glancing out at the brightness of the morning sun across the sand and sea.

"No," Christy said quickly. "But I want to learn how to be. The verse I've been trying to memorize and put into practice this month is 'Godliness with contentment is great gain.' It's 1 Timothy 6:6. Interesting, isn't it?" Christy took a handful of her hair and flipped it back. "We're both kind of learning the same thing: how to be happy where we are."

"What surprised me this week is how complicated life can be. Like with you and Todd. I thought my life would be so much easier if I had a boyfriend. But then I see how you two still have a lot of things to work out and how it takes a lot of time and energy. That means your life is still complicated, even though you have a boyfriend."

Christy laughed softly. "Uncle Bob once told me, 'If you think the grass is greener on the other side of the fence, try watering your own grass.'"

Sierra laughed. "That's what it's like, isn't it? Here I am, watching everyone else carry on with his or her life and wishing I was on the other side of the fence. You're right, Christy. I'm going to ask God to teach me how to live like that—godly with contentment and paying attention to my side of the fence."

"And don't forget to water your own grass!" Christy added.

"And watering my own grass," Sierra repeated.

They sat silently for a few moments in the large, quiet room. The rest of the household still wasn't stirring. Sierra knew she had found a rare treasure of a friend in Christy because they were able to sit together silently and it didn't feel awkward. The only other person she felt that level of comfort with was her Granna Mae.

"Do you feel like praying with me?" Sierra asked. "My mom and Granna Mae always pray with us, and, well, this seems like a good praying time."

"Sure." Christy closed her eyes, and the two friends welcomed the new day with heartfelt prayers of praise and a few requests. Sierra surrendered her jealousy to the Lord and asked Him to do one of His God-things between her and Tawni. Christy prayed for her aunt and uncle, and they prayed together for a swift healing for Todd and Uncle Bob.

Sierra was saying "Amen" when they heard someone come down the stairs. They both turned around to see Marti in a purple silk robe.

"Whatever are you two doing up so early?"

Sierra was about to say, "Just talking," but Christy answered first. "Praying."

"Oh, really, Christina. Don't be so flippant."

"I'm not. We were praying. For you and Uncle Bob," Christy said.

Marti seemed to brush off the comment and turned toward the kitchen. "I'm going to make some coffee. Do you drink coffee, Sierra?"

"No, but I'll have some tea if you happen to have any."

"Me, too," Christy said. "We'll come make it. As a matter of fact, we'll make the coffee, too. Why don't you go back to bed? We'll bring the coffee to you."

"Well!" Marti looked pleasantly surprised. "Now I know what they mean when they say 'Prayer works.'" She grinned at her own little joke. "I'll be upstairs. And you might want to bring a cup for your mother, Christy. She's going home this morning since Bob's coming out of the hospital today."

"We'll bring it right up," Christy said, leading Sierra into the kitchen. Christy pulled the coffee beans out of the pantry, but she didn't seem sure of what to do next.

"Do you know where the coffee grinder is?" Sierra asked.

"I'm not sure. My parents drink instant coffee. I don't know how to make this."

"Step aside," Sierra said. "I learned all about how to make the perfect cup of coffee from Granna Mae. Why don't you make the tea?"

They went to work searching for tea bags and the coffee grinder. Once the coffee began to brew, Sierra collected the cream and sugar and put them on a tray.

"Let's cut up some fruit," Christy suggested. "And bagels are probably in the freezer. Yep, here they are. Let's take breakfast to everyone in bed!"

Fifteen minutes later, they were heading upstairs, carefully balancing their two full trays and trying not to giggle. Everything had seemed funny to them as they had prepared their love offering in the kitchen. Christy had even snatched some flowers from a bouquet on the dining room table and put them in juice glasses, one vase for each tray.

"Room service," Christy said cheerfully as she opened the door to Marti's bedroom with her elbow.

Marti was back in bed with the covers folded all nice and neat as if she had been patiently waiting for them. She reminded Sierra of Granna Mae, except that Marti's comment was unlike anything Granna Mae would say. "What took you so long? You brought the nonfat creamer, I hope."

"Yes, it's all here," Christy said, patiently unloading the coffee cup and accoutrements onto Marti's nightstand. "Would you like some fruit or a bagel?"

"No. Your mother is in my shower, so you can leave her coffee over there. What's the rest of this for?"

"We thought we would serve breakfast in bed to all the women in the household," Christy said, still smiling. "Are you sure you don't want some fruit?"

"Well, maybe just a slice of that cantaloupe."

The other women were more appreciative. As Tawni took the coffee mug from Sierra, she said, "This smells wonderful. Thanks. Have the guys called yet?"

"Not that I know of," Sierra said. "It's still early."

"Jeremy wants to take me to some restaurant he likes in Laguna Beach. We'll probably make a day of it."

"That sounds fun," Katie said.

"He's such an incredible guy," Tawni said, sipping the coffee and looking as if her mind were still in a dream. "I can't believe I met him."

Sierra was about to let her feelings start bubbling up when Christy said, "Tell us what you like about him."

"Well, you know him, Christy. He's strong-minded and yet tender about so many things. He's a deeply committed Christian, which makes all the difference in the world from the last few guys I've been interested in. He treats me like an equal, and at the same time he does little things to let me know he cares about me."

Sierra was about to interject one of her typically rude comments, but something stopped her. The Holy Spirit, maybe? She realized that if Katie were talking about Antonio or Christy about Todd, Sierra would be making all kinds of affirming comments to let her friends know how happy she was that they had found great guys. Why couldn't she be that supportive of her sister?

"I'm really happy for you, Tawni," Sierra said, her voice and expression reflecting her sincerity.

"You are?"

"Yes, I am. I think he's a dream come true, and I'm really glad you met him."

"Thanks," Tawni said.

Sierra glanced at Christy out of the corner of her eye and caught a slight wink her heart-friend was sending her way—silent applause for this not-so-minor victory.

## chapter sixteen

The rest of the day filled up quickly. Christy's mom left, Marti went to the hospital with Todd and Christy to bring Uncle Bob home, Tawni and Jeremy left at 11:00 for their big lunch date, and Sierra and Katie hung out at the beach with the rest of the bunch. Doug and Tracy didn't show up. Heather said they were spending the day making plans.

Sierra decided it was time to "water her own grass" and put her whole heart into teaching herself to surf. She bravely asked to borrow Todd's battered, orange surfboard, and for more than two hours, she tried to ignore her aching arms as she paddled out again and again. Finally, she caught a wave and managed to stand up and keep her balance all the way to shore. No one saw her. No one was waiting to applaud. But she knew she had done something she had always wanted to do, and the feeling it gave her was, in Doug's word, "awesome."

After a short nap in the sun, she challenged Antonio to a game of paddle ball. They went down to the water and began to throw a ball to each other, catching it with Velcro-lined mitts. Katie had taken Todd's board back out and was hard at work trying to catch a good one. Sierra decided to be brave and ask Antonio if she could borrow his board. She took it out like a pro and bobbed about with Katie, waiting for the afternoon swell to pick up.

They talked, paddled, floated, and laughed. Sierra knew she would never forget this afternoon, not because anything spectacular was happening but simply because she felt so fully alive. Her heart felt fresh and clean, and she loved the sense of freedom the ocean gave her.

Katie began talking about Antonio. Sierra decided to bring up Randy and the date next Friday night.

"Good choice on the corsage suggestion," Katie said. "When I went to the prom, my date gave me this hilarious green carnation. It looked like a head of lettuce!"

"I don't know why I said peach. I should have said white roses. They would go with anything."

"Peach is a nice, neutral color. Green, on the other hand, doesn't match anything. What a disaster that night was! You know what, Sierra? If I knew in high school how much fun I was going to have in college, I wouldn't have been so paranoid about trying to get a boyfriend. Enjoy yourself, and don't make any bad memories with a guy just for the sake of having a date."

"I'll remember that," Sierra said.

"Whoa," Katie said, getting into position on her board. "Here comes the one we've been waiting for." She began to paddle furiously, and Sierra followed right behind. Katie was faster—she caught the wave, stood up, and rode to shore. It all seemed symbolic to Sierra as she watched and waited for the next decent wave. Katie was older, so of course she was ahead of Sierra and deserved to catch the wave. Somehow it didn't bother Sierra, being the one to watch and wait for waves and for romance.

She had more opportunities to watch and wait that night when everyone gathered around an open fire pit at the beach. Christy led them all to a certain fire pit she'd picked out of all the open ones on the beach. The group spread their blankets, and the guys started a fire. There was some teasing of Todd, telling him to stand back and have a beach towel ready in case the pit blew up. Sierra didn't think the jokes were funny, having been at the house and seen the accident. But the seriousness seemed to have passed now that Todd was doing better and Bob had come home from the hospital. He had gone right to bed, Christy told them. But he had invited everyone over for breakfast the next morning, so he must be feeling better.

The sun was making its grand exit as they gathered around the fire pit, and Sierra was glad she had worn her sweatshirt. She sat next to Christy, who offered her the other half of her blanket and said, "Anyone want to roast marshmallows?"

A chorus of cheers echoed from around the campfire.

"Then you get to untwist your own coat hanger," Christy said, pulling a handful from a bag and passing them around.

Todd, who was sitting on the other side of Christy, was

right in the path of the smoke. He sat there about two minutes before coming around and sitting on the other side of Sierra.

"Would you like me to move so you can sit next to Christy?" Sierra asked.

"No, this is fine. Pass me a couple of marshmallows, will you?" He took them from Sierra and slid them onto his coat hanger. "Okay," he challenged. "First one to brown a marshmallow nice and even all around without burning is the winner."

Sierra promptly untwisted her coat hanger, grabbed two marshmallows, and entered the competition.

"What's the prize?" Antonio asked.

"The knowledge that you're the victor," Todd said.

"You Americans are so contemplative," Antonio said.

"You mean 'competitive,'" Katie said.

"Oh, you've noticed it, too?" Antonio grinned at her.

For apparently the first time, it occurred to Katie that Antonio had a superb command of the English language and had been teasing her all along. "You've been having a good time with me, haven't you?" she said.

"Of course. I thought you were having a good time, too."

"I mean with your words. You've been mixing things up just to—"

"Just to win your attention. And it's worked nicely, hasn't it?"

Before Katie could toss him a quick retort, Doug and Tracy, with their arms around each other, approached the group. Doug was carrying a guitar case, and Tracy had a plastic grocery bag.

"Marshmallow reinforcements!" Doug called out.

Todd reached across Sierra and grabbed some marshmallows from Christy's bag. "Excuse me," he said, and before Doug could see where they were coming from, Todd pelted him with flying marshmallows.

"Stand back, Trace," Doug said, holding his guitar case in front of them. "I'll protect you!"

"Oh, you guys, look!" Sierra said, pulling her twirling stick from the fire. "We almost have a winner here." Her marshmallows were nearly brown all the way around. Now came the tricky part of toasting the sagging underside before it oozed off the coat hanger and into the fire.

"We may have an early winner, folks," Todd said, sticking his marshmallows back into the fire. "But not without some competition."

Christy, who had been quietly roasting her marshmallows, now pulled her hanger from the fire and said, "Did you say competition?" As she said it, both her nearly perfect marshmallows began to droop beyond rescuing. She quickly grabbed them with her fingers. The sticky goo dripped down her hand as she tried to get it into her mouth. Christy's eyes grew wide, and she pointed to the fire. Sierra looked in time to see her two perfect balls of sugar bursting into flames.

"I'm still in," Sierra said. "Second try. Somebody hand me a marshmallow."

For the next half hour, the gang roasted all the marsh-

mallows in Christy's bag and Tracy's two bags. There
were plenty of flaming marshmallow balls dropped into
the fire, and in the end, Tawni was the winner with the
most evenly roasted marshmallows. Sierra realized she
shouldn't have been surprised. Tawni had the diligence to
stick to it and wait patiently. Diligence and patience were
two of her sister's good qualities that Sierra had never
noticed much.

"You've kept us in suspense long enough," Christy
finally said to Tracy and Doug. "When's the wedding?
Did you set a date?"

"After spending the whole day with both mothers, you
better believe we did," Doug said. "August 22, and you're
all invited."

"This August?" Heather squawked.

"That was the only day all summer we could agree on.
And if I go to graduate school," Doug explained, "we
don't want to wait until next summer or try to squeeze in
a wedding during Christmas break."

"Wow!" Todd said. "Wow!"

"I think it sounds perfect," Christy said. "I'm really
happy and excited for both of you."

"Good," Tracy said, "because I have a favor to ask.
Actually, Doug and I have a favor to ask you and Todd.
Christy, will you be my maid of honor?"

"And Todd," Doug picked up, "you're the best man—
okay, dude?"

"Wait a minute, wait a minute," Todd said. "This isn't
like auditioning parts for a school play. This is your

wedding we're talking about. With all your family and all your friends, are you sure you want us?"

"Of course. We've already talked it through," Tracy said.

"With both mothers," Doug added. "So you know the arrangement has been sanctified."

"I'm honored," Todd said. "Of course I'll be your best man."

"And I'd love to be your maid of honor," Christy said.

"We haven't agreed on all the other attendants yet, but we're going to figure out a way to have all you guys in our wedding somehow. If nothing else, we really want all of you to be there."

"We wouldn't miss it for anything," Heather said.

"So, Doug," Todd said, poking the logs in the fire and watching them tumble, shooting off dozens of tiny, red firecrackers, "exactly what does a best man do?"

"Isn't he the guy who kidnaps the groom the night before the wedding and has him dyed fuchsia all over?" Larry said.

"Wait a minute," Doug said. "I'm not planning on being kidnapped. Todd, as my best man, you're supposed to protect me from maniacs like Larry."

Sierra couldn't picture Todd having much control over Larry, or anyone being able to stop him—except perhaps Gisele. She appeared to be his soft spot.

"That's the beauty of it," Larry said. "No groom ever plans to be kidnapped. Consider it a parting gift from us bachelors."

"I don't know," Doug said. "My idea to elope is starting to sound better and better."

"Can you believe you guys are getting married?" Katie asked. "I can't."

"Well, try to imagine it," Doug said. "Because we are." He put his arm around Tracy and squeezed her tightly. Tracy's face looked radiant in the glow of the campfire.

Sierra gazed into the warm embers and made a wish. Inside her heart, she wished that one day she would be as deeply in love as Tracy and Doug and that her love would be as pure as theirs.

# chapter seventeen

WHEN THE GROUP GATHERED FOR BREAKFAST the next morning, they found everything set up for them in the formal dining room. A caterer had been hired to serve the large group, wedged around the table.

"Don't look so shocked," Katie said as she took a seat next to Sierra. "This is pretty typical of Marti. I'm sure it's her idea of a welcome home party for Bob."

"It's pretty fancy, don't you think?" Sierra whispered back.

"Of course! The flashier the better in Marti's book. You should see this place during Christmas."

Bob sat at the head of the table, looking pale but smiling. The gauze bandages came up his left arm and covered half of his neck and his ear. Sierra knew he must be in pain. With Marti's help, he was bolstered up in the chair, making a rather regal appearance despite the handicap.

Once the orange juice had been poured into the crystal glasses, Bob tapped the side of his with a spoon. Then he held up the glass, inviting a toast.

Everyone grew quiet, and Bob said, "Guess I missed most of the party this week. Sorry about that. I was probably looking forward to it more than you all were."

A ripple of laughter moved down the table.

"This makes up for it," Larry said from his position at the other end of the table. Sierra noticed his plate was heaped with eggs, sausages, and pancakes. Gisele sat on his right with only a few slices of fruit and a pineapple muffin on her plate. It reminded Sierra of a picture in her nephew's nursery rhyme book of Jack Sprat and his wife, only in reverse.

"I wanted you all to be together so I could make an announcement. I wish Margaret had stayed," Bob said, looking at Christy. "You tell your mom and dad everything I say, okay?"

Christy looked solemn and nodded. Sierra wondered if this was going to be some big announcement about the family inheritance. She felt as if she had stepped into a remake of a Gothic mystery movie. All they needed was a change of wardrobe, a rainstorm with lightning, and a silver candelabra on the mantle.

But it wasn't that kind of atmosphere at all. The morning sun flooded through the front windows, piercing the crystals on the chandelier above them and sending dozens of ballerina rainbows across the table. The centerpiece bouquet was laden with large, white garde- nias. Their fragrance floated through the air, intoxicating each of the guests with the sweetness.

Bob, sitting majestically before them, spoke with a

lightheartedness that fit the joy permeating the room. Clearing his throat, he said, "What happened a few days ago caused me to take my life more seriously than I ever have before. I did a lot of what you would probably call soul-searching and have come to a decision. That is, I've realized . . . or rather, it seemed the right time to . . ." His voice faltered. "What I mean is . . ."

"You got saved!" Katie blurted out.

All eyes were on Bob, waiting for his response. A wide smile broke across his face. "Thank you, Katie. That's what happened. I got saved."

Bedlam broke out. Christy, Todd, Katie, and Doug shot up from their seats like rockets, shouting and laughing and trying to hug Bob without disturbing the bandages. Marti was frantically trying to keep them from touching him. Larry was standing at the end of the table applauding and hooting like a football fan whose favorite team had just won the Super Bowl. Tracy and Heather got in line to hug Bob, while Gisele and the others joined Larry in clapping and cheering.

Sierra sprang to her feet and went over to hug Bob, too, even though she barely knew him. She realized how long Todd and Christy had been waiting for this day, and she shared in their excitement. She couldn't help but feel a part of it.

Tears were streaming down Bob's cheeks. It was rich to see a man cry over his welcome into the kingdom. When Sierra hugged him, she impulsively planted a little kiss on his cheek. Her lips tasted the salt of his tears. "Welcome to the family," she whispered.

"And now the toast," Larry said in his booming voice. He stood at the other end of the table with his juice glass lifted in the air.

Bob struggled to stand up, with Todd supporting his one arm and Sierra bracing the other. Bob lifted his glass. Making eye contact, one by one, with each of his guests, he said, "My brothers and sisters in Christ, here's to eternity."

Everyone cheered—except Marti.

She stood at the appropriate time, but Sierra noticed that she used the opportunity to step to the corner of the room and issue instructions to the woman serving their breakfast. A moment later, the server returned with a fresh basket of muffins and walked around trying to offer them to everyone.

No one accepted. Everyone was too busy cheering and talking.

Bob sat down and told how all the men from the morning Bible study had come to visit him in the hospital, one at a time. "None of them said what I thought he would say. They each just came and sat with me, and most of them asked if they could pray with me. I kept thinking about things Todd had told me over the years, about needing to repent and yield my life to Christ, to ask Him to be my Savior. I never thought I needed a Savior before. But when your life is almost taken from you, I guess you stop believing in luck and start hoping there really is a Savior."

"Oh, there is," Christy said, her eyes still brimming with tears. "And you found Him, Uncle Bob."

"Actually, I think He found me."

"Didn't take too much for Him to get your full attention, now did it?" Doug said with a laugh.

Bob tipped his juice glass in Doug's direction. "You know," he said, "I tried to explain it to Marti last night, and I couldn't find the words." He cast a loving glance at his wife.

Her expression was ice with a painted-on smile.

"I don't know what happened, but I'm a different man inside."

The doorbell rang, and Doug, who was closest to the entryway, went to answer the door. A moment later, he stepped back into the dining room with three large suitcases. "The case of the lost luggage is solved, Tawni."

"Oh, that's perfect!" she said. "My plane leaves for home in two hours, and now they deliver my luggage."

Doug carried the suitcases back to the front door, and Sierra noticed Todd casting his silver-blue eyes first at Christy, then at Bob. He leaned toward Bob and said, "What once was lost, now is found."

Christy echoed Todd's ecstatic grin at her uncle.

Without a word, Bob lifted his glass and clinked it with Todd's and then with Christy's. "What once was lost, now is found," Bob repeated.

Sierra knew they weren't referring to Tawni's luggage.

# chapter eighteen

O N EASTER SUNDAY, SIERRA SAT NEXT TO Granna Mae on the hard pew in Granna Mae's old church. Tall, white Easter lilies lined the steps up to the altar, their heady fragrance filling Sierra with all the reminders of spring, new life, and the miracle of the resurrection.

Her heart was full this morning. It seemed so much had happened during the past week that pointed to this celebration of Christ conquering death. On the final hymn, Sierra helped Granna Mae stand, and with passion, Sierra sang alongside her grandmother: "Christ the Lord is risen today!"

The warm glow of the week and the holiness of the Easter morning service stayed with Sierra all day. She cheerfully helped her mother set the table after church for their big family dinner. Her oldest brother, Wesley, was up from Corvallis, and her brother Cody; his wife, Katrina; and their three-year-old son, Tyler, were there, too.

When they were all seated at the long table in the dining room, Sierra's dad stood to pray. When he sat down,

Sierra popped up and lifted her water glass. "I would like to propose a toast," she said.

"Since when did our family start giving toasts?" Wes asked.

"Since your sister was influenced by a certain wealthy Uncle Bob in Newport Beach," Tawni told him.

"I would like to say thank you to God for my family, who are all believers. I don't ever want to take you for granted," Sierra said. "Here's to eternity."

The group didn't jump in as eagerly as the bunch at Bob and Marti's breakfast. But Granna Mae led the way, holding her glass up to Sierra and saying, "To eternity!"

Sierra still felt extra cheerful when she returned to school on Monday. Amy was the first person she saw in the parking lot that morning.

"No fair!" Amy said, holding her arm next to Sierra's. "You're so tan. Look at you!"

"Well, that can happen to a person when she lies on the beach in Southern California for days on end," Sierra said, enjoying the attention.

"I want to hear all about it," Amy said. "I can summarize my Easter vacation for you in two words: BOR-ING."

"Are you doing anything after school today?" Sierra asked. "I need to shop for a new dress." She knew Amy would be a good companion since they had similar taste in clothes. Sierra had never met anyone who dressed the way she did, until she met Amy.

"You, too?" Amy said, as she and Sierra walked together through the parking lot. "I spent three days shopping with Vicki last week in search of the perfect semi-formal outfit. You know, don't you, that she asked Randy to go with her to some benefit dinner this Friday? I can't remember if I told you before you left."

Sierra stopped at the last row of cars, her heart pounding. "She asked Randy to go with her?"

Amy stopped alongside Sierra and nodded. "The poor guy is such a nervous wreck. He made me go shopping with him last week, too. I finally talked him into renting a tux. You should see him in it. He looks so cute! Like a waiter. I didn't tell him that, though." Amy looked closely at Sierra. "How come your tan just left your face?"

"I'm surprised. That's all."

"I thought Randy said he told you. Didn't he ask your advice on what kind of flowers to buy for the corsage?"

"Yes," Sierra said, finding her voice and feeling foolish, "he did. He came into work the day before I left and asked me."

A flash of understanding came across Amy's face. "Oh, Sierra, you didn't think he was asking you to go, did you?"

Sierra bit her lower lip and squinted her eyes to keep any stupid tears from exposing her. She didn't have a voice to answer Amy at the moment.

"Oh, dear," Amy said, leaning against the nearest car.

The parking lot had filled up, and dozens of students were hurrying past them to class.

"That's right. He made a big deal at the park about going to Mama Bear's to talk to you, didn't he?"

Sierra found her wits again and grabbed Amy by the

arm. She leaned close and said, "Amy, promise me you won't say anything to Randy or Vicki or anybody about this."

Amy looked startled at Sierra's sudden, dramatic request.

"Promise me," Sierra breathed. "It would kill me to have Randy find out. He deserves to have a great time, and I don't want to send any messages that might give him the wrong idea. Okay? It was just my own ridiculous misunderstanding. Promise me you won't say anything."

"I promise," Amy said solemnly. "You can trust me. I can keep secrets."

"Good," Sierra said, letting go of Amy's arm.

Just then the bell rang, and they took off running to their first class.

# *chapter nineteen*

S IERRA MADE IT THROUGH THE WEEK WITHOUT any awkward encounters with Randy. He seemed preoccupied with Vicki anyhow. Amy apparently kept Sierra's secret, which made Sierra feel loyal to Amy and appreciative of her friendship. Amy appeared equally interested in letting their friendship develop, because she invited Sierra to go to dinner at Amy's uncle's Italian restaurant downtown on Friday night.

"Just us girls," Amy said.

"You mean we leave the dogs at home?" Sierra asked.

"You are referring to Brutus and Peanut, aren't you?"

"Of course? Who else?"

"Oh, nobody. But you're right. I don't think my uncle would like having a couple of canines there. He said dinner tonight would be his treat. Our reservations are at eight. I'll drive, okay?"

Sierra agreed and tried to explain to Amy how much she appreciated the invitation.

"Don't worry about it," Amy said. "I would have asked you even if the Randy mix-up hadn't happened. Be ready by 7:30, okay?"

Sierra was ready early. The spring evening carried the fragrance of a mixed bouquet wafting from the trees surrounding Granna Mae's house. Sierra stepped outside onto the big porch that wrapped around the front. The white porch swing called to her: *Come, sit here and sway with me in the evening breeze.* Sierra obliged, nestling on the thickly padded seat her mom had made the week Sierra was gone. Freshly potted plants lined the porch railing. Mom had jokingly referred to the petunias, primroses, and pansies as her "three P's in a pot."

Swaying back and forth on the swing, Sierra drew in a deep breath of the spring sweetness around her. Two squirrels scampered across the telephone line, and a plump robin hopped across the front yard, looking for dinner.

*Why do I feel so . . . What is this feeling? Happy? Settled? Happily settled into life in Portland. That's it,* Sierra thought. *No, a better word would be "content." What was Christy's verse last week? "Godliness with contentment is great gain." That's what it is. I'm content.*

Sierra certainly felt she had gained a lot. It had been great to see the gang last week, but now she knew this was where she needed to find new friends—friends her own age who were experiencing the same things she was, even if those things were crazy misunderstandings over corsages and dates. She wanted to take her time growing up, and she wanted to embrace all of it, good and bad.

She felt more certain than ever that God had His hand on her life and that He was working everything out the way He designed it to be. With a push of her feet against the wooden planks under the swing, Sierra rocked with an even, steady rhythm, the way a clock ticks off the passing seconds.

As she did, the thoughts ticked off in her settled mind. Trusting God in this big way made it hard to be jealous of Tawni or Vicki or anyone. Why would Sierra want what someone else had if that wasn't what God had decided was best for her? Didn't He know best? Wouldn't He be faithful to work out His plan in her life? Sierra eagerly desired to slip into motion with that plan and not resist or hinder it in any way.

As she was letting these soothing thoughts lull her in the swing, a car pulled up in front of the house. She knew it wasn't Amy's. Sierra peeked between the row of blooming flowers in the clay pots and saw a guy in a tuxedo coming up the front walkway with something in his hand.

*Randy?* "Hi," Sierra called as he stepped up to the porch.

Randy looked startled. "Oh, hi. I didn't see you." He ambled toward her.

"You look terrific," Sierra said, a grin spreading across her face.

"Thanks. I feel like a penguin."

Sierra laughed. "You don't look like one."

"Here. I wanted to drop this off for you." He held out a peach-colored tea rose tucked in a sprig of baby's breath and wrapped in green florist paper. "It's to say thanks for the advice on the corsage."

"You didn't have to do this," Sierra said, receiving the flower and drawing in its scent.

"I wanted to. You're a good friend, Sierra. I appreciate you."

"Thanks, Randy." She could feel her cheeks warm at his words.

"Well—" He let out a deep breath. "I guess I better go."

"Just a minute," Sierra said, getting up from the swing and going toward him. Randy looked even more nervous as she came closer. "Don't worry, Randy. I'm only going to fix your tie. Hold still." She tugged on the right side of the bow, wiggling it until both sides were even. "There. Now you're ready."

Sierra noticed two trickles of sweat coursing from his temple down his cheek. "Relax," Sierra said with a smile. "You look great, and I know you'll have a wonderful time."

The screen door swung open, and Tawni appeared with the cordless phone in her hand. "I found her, Jeremy," Tawni said. "She was on the front porch with . . . Randy?"

He raised his hand in a stiff hello. "I was on my way out," he said.

"You look absolutely fantastic!" Tawni cooed. Then, turning her attention back to Jeremy on the other end of the phone, she said, "It's just one of Sierra's friends dressed up for the prom or something."

Randy mouthed the words "See you later" and waved at Sierra as he galloped down the steps and dashed to his car.

"Thanks for the flower!" Sierra called after him.

Tawni was holding the phone out to her and said, "Here. You speak with him. I don't understand what Jeremy is talking about. He says he thought you knew."

"Knew what?"

Tawni pushed the phone into her hand, and Sierra put the receiver to her ear. "Hi, Jeremy. What's up?"

"Flowers, huh?" Jeremy said. "Maybe my brother is up against stiffer competition than he thought."

Sierra gave Tawni a puzzled look. Tawni held up her hands and said, "I told him I didn't know anything about it."

"Do you want to rewind a bit, Jeremy? What are you and Tawni talking about?"

"I'm planning to come up there in a few weeks. Did Tawni tell you?"

"No, not yet. That's great. I'm sure you'll like meeting our family."

"Well, I was hoping you would like to meet someone in my family. But then, he tells me you already know him."

"Who?" Sierra asked, switching the phone to her other hand. She put the rose on the swing and shrugged her shoulders at Tawni.

"Do you remember a certain letter Katie sent to you a while back?" Jeremy asked. "I gave the letter to her after my brother gave it to me. It was the only way he could think of to contact you after your encounter at the airport in London."

"Paul?!" Sierra felt an invisible hand push her against one of the porch pillars. "You're Paul's brother?"

"He was pretty shocked when he figured it out, too. I told him about Tawni and then mentioned she had a sister named Sierra."

"And what did he say?" Sierra asked.

"He figured it had to be you. He told me the whole story. The money you loaned him at the pay phone in London. Sitting by you on the flight home. Getting your luggage mixed up. And something about his calling you a daffodil queen and your getting upset and writing a flaming letter telling him he wasn't sincere."

Sierra closed her eyes and wished for the hundredth time that she hadn't so impulsively mailed that letter. If there was one thing she wished she could learn, it would be to keep her mouth shut. Or, in this case, to keep her words inside her head instead of committing them to paper.

"That was . . . it didn't really . . . I wasn't . . ." She fumbled to find a combination of words to explain. "It was kind of a mix-up. In the end, he brought my grandma flowers. I never got to thank him. Would you tell him thanks for me?"

"Sure. Is there anything else you would like me to tell him? I already told him that I saw you surf last week. That didn't seem to surprise him."

"Why should it?" Sierra challenged.

"That's right. Nothing about you or your sister should surprise me, should it?"

"What about your brother? Will he have any surprises for me?"

"What do you mean?"

"He's not dating Jalene any more, is he?"

"No, that broke up months ago. The way I understood it, you had something to do with it. At least that's what I understand from Paul and my mom. You're becoming a little legend with our family."

Sierra suppressed a giggle. Here she thought Paul had long forgotten about her and their conversation on the plane, and he had actually told his parents about her.

"Well, tell him hi for me."

"Okay. Anything else?"

"Tell him that godliness with contentment is great gain."

"What?"

"Never mind," Sierra said, catching the strange expression on her sister's face. "Just tell him I hope he's doing well."

"Okay. I'll tell him. And hey, when I come up in a couple of weeks, maybe the four of us can get together or something. Meanwhile, can you put Tawni back on the line?"

Sierra handed the phone to Tawni, who covered the mouthpiece and said, "I still don't understand."

"I'll explain the whole thing later," Sierra promised. She settled onto the cushion on the swing and drew in the rose's delicate fragrance.

As the porch swing gently rocked her, ticking away the moments, Sierra found an irrepressible smile had captured her lips. Her thoughts whirled with all the wild, romantic, wonderful possibilities that might be waiting for her down the road. Then, into the air she whispered to the One who already knew what she was thinking, "Oh, don't I wish!"

# Two Captivating Series from Robin Jones Gunn

## THE CHRISTY MILLER SERIES

## THE SIERRA JENSEN SERIES